P9-CQH-676

Josh wasn't sure about anything where Rebel McCade was concerned.

He truly wasn't used to such an open, breezy woman. One who said exactly what she thought and didn't play by the usual rules. Or even seem aware of them. Who woke up in the morning in such a cheerful mood.

Most women of Josh's acquaintance were encountered in crowded boardrooms or at high-impact meetings. Occasionally they were met, and sometimes pursued, at formal cocktail parties or lavish dinners. Not once in recent memory had one of them been thrust on him in the middle of a shipwreck. Small wonder he felt a little out of his depth where Rebel McCade was concerned!

Dear Reader,

Those long days of summer sunshine are just around the corner—and Special Edition has six fabulous new books to start off the season right!

This month's THAT'S MY BABY! title is brought to you by the wonderful Janis Reams Hudson. *His Daughter's Laughter* tells the poignant tale of a widowed dad, his fragile little girl and the hope they rediscover when one extraordinary woman touches their lives.

June is the month of wedding bells—or in some cases, wedding blues. Be sure to check out the plight of a runaway bride who leaves one groom behind, only to discover another when she least expects it in *Cowboy's Lady*—the next installment in Victoria Pade's ongoing A RANCHING FAMILY miniseries. And there's more romance on the way with award-winning author Ruth Wind's *Marriage Material*— book one in THE LAST ROUNDUP, a new cross-line series with Intimate Moments about three brothers who travel the rocky road to love in a small Colorado town.

And speaking of turbulent journeys, in *Remember Me?* Jennifer Mikels tells a passionate love story about an amnesiac woman who falls for the handsome hero who rescues her from a raging rainstorm. Also in June, Shirley Larson presents *That Wild Stallion*—an emotional Western that's sure to tug your heartstrings.

Finally, *New York Times* bestselling author Ellen Tanner Marsh lives up to her reputation with *A Doctor in the House*, her second Silhouette title. It's all work and no play for this business executive until he meets his match in the form of one feisty Southern beauty in the Florida Keys!

I hope you enjoy all our summer stories this month!

Sincerely,

Tara Gavin
Senior Editor

Please address questions and book requests to:
Silhouette Reader Service
U.S.: 3010 Walden Ave., P.O. Box 1325, Buffalo, NY 14269
Canadian: P.O. Box 609, Fort Erie, Ont. L2A 5X3

ELLEN TANNER MARSH

A DOCTOR IN THE HOUSE

Silhouette ®

SPECIAL EDITION ®

Published by Silhouette Books
America's Publisher of Contemporary Romance

If you purchased this book without a cover you should be aware
that this book is stolen property. It was reported as "unsold and
destroyed" to the publisher, and neither the author nor the
publisher has received any payment for this "stripped book."

To my son, Zachary, who loves the Keys.

SILHOUETTE BOOKS

ISBN 0-373-24110-0

A DOCTOR IN THE HOUSE

Copyright © 1997 by Ellen Tanner Marsh

All rights reserved. Except for use in any review, the reproduction
or utilization of this work in whole or in part in any form by any
electronic, mechanical or other means, now known or hereafter
invented, including xerography, photocopying and recording, or in
any information storage or retrieval system, is forbidden without
the written permission of the editorial office, Silhouette Books,
300 East 42nd Street, New York, NY 10017 U.S.A.

All characters in this book have no existence outside the imagination of
the author and have no relation whatsoever to anyone bearing the
same name or names. They are not even distantly inspired by any individual
known or unknown to the author, and all incidents are pure invention.

This edition published by arrangement with Harlequin Books S.A.

® and TM are trademarks of Harlequin Books S.A., used under license.
Trademarks indicated with ® are registered in the United States Patent
and Trademark Office, the Canadian Trade Marks Office and in other
countries.

Printed in U.S.A.

Books by Ellen Tanner Marsh

Silhouette Special Edition

A Family of Her Own #978
A Doctor in the House #1110

ELLEN TANNER MARSH's

love of animals almost cost her readers the pleasure of experiencing her immensely popular romances. However, Ellen's dream of becoming a veterinarian was superseded by her desire to write. So, after college, she took her pen and molded her ideas and notes into full-length stories. Her combination of steamy prose and fastidious historical research eventually landed her on the *New York Times* bestseller list with her very first novel, *Reap the Savage Wind*. She now has over three million copies of her books in print, is translated into four languages and is the recipient of a *Romantic Times* Lifetime Achievement Award.

When Ellen is not at her word processor, she is showing her brindled Great Dane, raising birds and keeping the grass cut on the family's four-acre property. She is married to her high-school sweetheart and lives with him and her two young sons, Zachary and Nicolas, in South Carolina.

HOW TO CURE AN ALL-WORK, NO-PLAY MILLIONAIRE:

The Subject:
Josh Alden, tireless tycoon

The Ailment:
Too many long hours spent at the office

Symptoms:
1. Suffering confirmed bachelor syndrome.
2. Socially challenged: extreme low levels of "having fun."

The Cure:
Rebel McCade, feisty free spirit

Prescription:
Lots of smiles, lots of laughter…lots of love

Warning:
All-work, no-play millionaires are difficult
to cure–particularly in one week's time.
Radical measures are sometimes necessary….

Chapter One

The rain was coming down in sheets. Whipped by the gale, it blew furiously against the slicker of the woman hunkered beside the sputtering motor of her boat.

"Shoot." Not the earthy expletive Rebel McCade would have normally used, but she'd promised Pop she'd cut down on her cussing now that Lee was home from school.

Scowling, she drew the collar of the bright yellow slicker tightly about her throat. Cold water dripped down her neck, anyway.

"Heck, shoot and darn."

The dog in the bow lifted its head and whined.

"Yeah, I know. I'm cold, too. Not much we can do about it."

Her blue eyes skimmed the white-capped water. Nothing could change as quickly as the ocean, she thought. Nothing. Azure, sun-drenched and warm as a bathtub one minute, storm tossed and gray the next.

"And we're stuck smack-dab in the middle of it."

Not that she was worried. Only wet and cold. And starving. Like the dog, no doubt. Sure, they could have been home in time for dinner even with the weather being so bad, but something had gone and gunked up their fuel line. Now Rebel's little skiff was puttering homeward at less than half its usual speed. With a little luck, she estimated they'd be crossing Hurricane Shoals in another hour, maybe two.

"Whoa, boy. Look over there!"

Almost uncannily the dog turned its head in the direction of Rebel's pointing finger. A sailboat had appeared through the curtain of rain. A big one, double masted, with running lights aglow. Sleek portholes indicated a number of cabins below. That meant a galley with food, a heater, dry towels...

"Man, that's a pretty sight!" Whooping joyfully, Rebel quickly changed course.

They must have spotted her at just about the same time. Someone was coming up on the sailboat's deck, braving the wind and the rain to wave a signal. Suddenly two men in flapping raincoats were visible.

The dog set up a barking at the sight of them. Laughing, Rebel put a finger to her lips. "No need to sound so desperate, you goober! We'll just say the engine's worse off than it is. They'll be sure to take us on board. Wait and see."

She wasn't worried about accepting help from strangers. Not boaters, anyway. Most of them were decent folk, more than willing to lend a hand when somebody's engine died.

Besides, Rebel was perfectly capable of looking after herself. And if she wasn't up to it, Yellow Dog certainly was.

Humming a little tune beneath her breath, she turned the rudder hard to port.

"Well, it's high time we ran into somebody! I certainly hope they can get us out of this mess!" Hands on his hips, Reardon Tate anxiously scanned the approaching skiff. "Oh, great. Only one chap aboard. How can he possibly be of any help?" Disappointed, he dashed the saltwater from his eyes. "What do you think? Should we trust him? Suppose he's a drug runner or something like that?"

Right, Josh Alden thought. Drug runners smuggling illicit wares in tiny, flat-bottomed boats. Trust a Tate to come up with something so farfetched. "Reardon, our situation isn't all that bad. We'll just ask him for a tow and—"

"Not that bad!" Reardon Tate stared at his cousin disbelievingly. "Have you lost your mind?

How can you say that? We've been without main power since noon! Our batteries are running low and—"

"And the storm should blow itself out in a couple more hours. Get a grip. We're not rounding the Cape of Good Hope or anything like that."

On the other hand, the way Reardon and his sister, Tracy, were acting, they might just as well be, Josh thought. Especially Tracy. For the past few hours she'd been carrying on as though the three of them were doomed.

Josh sighed and shook his head. Naturally a brand-new sailboat like this one was going to have a few kinks that needed working out. But at least they were still under way, with plenty of fuel left. And they were heading in the right direction, according to the compass. So why did Tracy and Reardon have to behave so damned hysterically?

They should have stayed home, Josh thought irritably. Tracy ought to be shopping right now, Reardon playing squash with old classmates from Yale. That was all either one of them was really good for.

He realized he was being unfair, but his mood didn't improve any. Looking up, he saw that the skiff had finally drawn alongside. Stooping, he began to uncoil one of the ropes. "Keep her into the wind, will you?" he called to his cousin.

Waves pummeled the skiff's bow. The figure in the stern had risen to catch the line. All Josh could see of the stranger's upturned face in the bleak light were huge eyes the color of slate, a slim, tipped-up nose and a point for a chin. The rest was concealed by a bright yellow raincoat.

Not tall enough to be a man, he thought. A boy, maybe? If so, what was he doing out in a storm like this in that bobbing cork of a boat?

"Ahoy!"

Wincing, Josh closed his eyes, then opened them again. *Ahoy* was the way Reardon signaled the guy? Where did he get *that* bull from, an Errol Flynn movie?

He cupped his own hands around his mouth. "Can you help us out up here?"

"What's wrong?" the kid in the skiff shouted back.

"We're lost!" Reardon yelled before Josh could answer.

Cool, Rebel thought. Even better than she'd hoped. Now they'd for sure invite her on board— and be thankful for her presence to boot. She addressed the tall one standing at the rail, the one whose dark eyes had been studying her all along. "Mind if I come up?"

"Be glad if you did."

"I've got a dog."

Josh hadn't noticed. Now his brows twitched together. The dog was half the size of a dairy calf, he noticed, but did he have any other choice? "Sure, why not?"

Reardon hurried over to him, glaring. "Are you out of your mind? A dog on Dad's new boat?"

Josh rounded on him. "Do you want to get to Key West or not?"

"Okay, okay." In the next moment Reardon let out a howl as the giant dog bounded onto the deck and shook water from its coat. Drool flew from its snout all over Reardon's slicker.

Grinning, Josh leaned down quickly to help the dog's owner aboard, but there was no need. Unmindful of the wildly canting deck, the man clambered over the railing with the same agility as the dog, shaking himself in much the same way, too, before lifting his head and grinning back at Josh.

"Thanks for the lift!"

Josh did a double take. This time he noticed more than the pointed chin and high, sculpted cheekbones. Up close he saw that the slate gray eyes were really blue, lit with good humor and sharp with intelligence. The rest might still be hidden by the bulky yellow slicker, but there was no doubt about it. He was guilty of a huge mistake. That sassy, smiling mouth didn't belong to a male any more than the rest of her did.

Before he could speak, Reardon shouldered him aside. "Glad you showed up. I'm Reardon Tate." He offered a hand in a gesture more relieved than friendly.

"Pleased to meet you."

"You—why, you're a girl!"

"Last I looked." Her voice was low and lilting. "I'm Rebel McCade."

Reardon, never one to be discreet, uttered a crack of laughter. "You're kidding! Wherever did you get a silly name like that?"

"Where'd you get yours?" she countered.

Reardon looked offended. He was, after all, intensely proud of his old family name.

"Come on," Josh interrupted with a growl. "Let's get out of the rain."

Rebel's dancing eyes turned to Reardon. "What's his problem?"

"Cousin Josh?"

"Yeah. Is he always so crabby?"

"Heavens, no." Reardon grinned, obviously deciding he liked her. "Sometimes he's a lot worse."

"Eeee!"

The shrill scream came from the direction of the hatchway.

Reardon rolled his eyes. "Oh, wonderful. We forgot about the dog."

"He won't hurt anyone," Rebel said quickly.

"Yes, I'm sure. But no one's told that to my sister."

Below in the cherry-paneled cabin, the big yellow dog had made himself comfortable on the galley mat. A puddle of dirty water pooled beneath him. The cabin smelled strongly of damp fur.

"Sorry," Rebel told the gorgeous brunette huddled in the dining booth. "He doesn't bite."

The woman's lovely nose wrinkled. "He certainly smells."

"I'll dry him off," Reardon volunteered much to Josh's amazement. "Tracy, this is Rebel."

The brunette's luscious mouth curled with distaste. "Do I look like I care what the creature's called?"

Rebel grinned. "Sorry, he means me. I'm Rebel McCade."

"You're kidding."

"That's exactly what your brother said. 'Fraid it's true."

Josh wondered if she ever stopped smiling. "Do you have a real name?"

Rebel made a face. A cute, little girl's face of utter disgust, Josh thought. "Scarlett Elizabeth. But nobody ever calls me that."

Or dared, apparently. Those unconsciously balled fists said so quite clearly.

Josh hid a smile. "Were your parents Margaret Mitchell fans by any chance?"

"Fanatics," Rebel answered gaily. "Can you think of a worse name for someone like me? *Scarlett.* Sheesh. I don't even have red hair."

No, it was very dark, and cut so short that it did give her a boyish look, although Josh couldn't honestly think of her that way anymore. He whirled to confront his cousin. "Reardon, how about a towel for Ms. McCade?"

"Coming right up. And you can come down off the bench, Trace. The dog doesn't bite."

"I'm fine where I am, thank you." Tracy's tone was frosty. "I hope you haven't forgotten our other problems, Reardon? Mainly the fact that we're lost?"

"Where were you bound?" Rebel asked, drawing back the hood of her slicker.

"We're out of Tampa on our way to Key West." Reardon's voice was muffled because he was rummaging in the linen cabinet.

"Key West!"

She sounded so startled that all of them turned to look at her.

"Is something wrong?" Josh asked.

"Well, considering you missed it..."

"Missed it!" Tracy sat bolt upright. "What do you mean, we've missed it?"

Rebel tipped her head aft. "I mean Key West is behind us, oh, thirty miles or so. You're east of Cudjoe Key by now."

Tracy gasped, then glared at her brother. "Reardon! You said— You told me—"

"I know, I know."

"My brother doesn't know a thing about navigation," she informed Rebel tartly.

Apparently not, Rebel silently agreed.

"This is Daddy's new boat. He bought it last week, and Reardon had the bright idea of sailing it to Miami for him. Now we're lost and the instruments don't work—"

"An electrical problem," Reardon interjected defensively. "Not my fault."

"So we've been tootling around in the wind and rain for hours and missed Key West completely!"

"Tracy, I told you—"

Over the heads of the arguing siblings, Rebel's eyes sought Josh's. He was leaning against a bulkhead, arms crossed in front of him, very still, very calm, as though he was used to waiting them out. Now that his chestnut hair was starting to dry, she saw that it was curly. She couldn't help smiling at him. She'd always been a sucker for men with curly hair. Besides, it didn't take a genius to figure out who was the most competent of the three.

"You could always turn around and go back," Rebel said.

"It'll be dark in a few hours, won't it?" Josh asked.

"Probably sooner, given the weather."

"Where's the nearest marina?"

Rebel paused a moment, considering. "Big Pine Key, but your best bet would be to head up to Marathon. I live nearby. I can get you there without a problem."

"How far away is that?" Tracy demanded.

"About an hour."

"An hour!"

"Maybe less," Rebel said soothingly.

"Told you not to make such a fuss," Reardon added smugly.

Tracy glared at him. She opened her mouth to resume arguing when a gust of wind suddenly battered the boat. The deck pitched roughly beneath them. She squealed and flew across the cabin to grab at Josh.

When his hands came up to steady Tracy, Rebel felt her breath catch in a funny little hitch. He looked so strong and protective that her heart seemed to sigh.

When the commotion died down, Rebel took the towel from Reardon and quickly knelt to dry her dog. The deck bucked beneath her, but she didn't seem to notice.

Tracy watched her with frightened eyes. "Aren't you scared?"

"Me? Nah."

"I—I wish I could say the same."

"It's all right, Trace," Josh said gently. "We'll be there before you know it."

Rebel's heart skipped another beat. She wasn't used to being around men who talked like that. Most of the men she knew—especially her father— were loud and coarse, and just as inclined to cuss someone out as offer comfort.

"Ms. McCade, will you take us to Marathon? Please?"

"Be glad to." She kept her tone light because Tracy was obviously scared. So was her brother, even though he was manfully trying to hide it. Well, who could really blame them? They weren't the first tourists Rebel had plucked out of the ocean in her twenty-six years of living on Gasparilla Key, a tiny island lying just across the bay from Marathon. In fact, she'd run into more than her share of them—folks who didn't know enough about the boats they handled, who'd misjudged the weather, the tides, the lay of the channels, who couldn't quite believe that the placid bay or the Gulf Stream could turn so ugly so fast. This is *Florida,* for cripes sake, they always said when trying to come to grips with what had happened.

"Where were you headed, Ms. McCade?"

Rebel used Josh's question as an excuse to take another look at him. She'd already decided that she liked looking at him—a lot. He was older than his cousin and, in Rebel's humble opinion, definitely more handsome.

Reardon Tate was one of those classically good-looking specimens you could always find splashed across the pages of glossy fashion magazines. Even though most women preferred guys like that, Rebel had to admit that she liked Josh's rugged looks a whole lot better. His features were all hollows and planes, as though they'd been carved from granite, his chin square with a heart-thumpingly gorgeous cleft in the center. His eyes were gray, and his chestnut hair extremely curly, even though it still clung damply to his face and neck. He'd peeled off his soaking jacket while Rebel was drying the dog, revealing a wide chest encased in a worn navy sweatshirt.

With difficulty she remembered that he'd asked her a question. She closed her mouth with a snap, certain that it had been hanging open like a dumb-struck teenager's.

"I was on my way to Gasparilla Key," she explained. "That's just off Marathon."

There was a map of Florida spread out on the table. Rebel put her finger on the spot. Josh leaned down to take a closer look, and their bodies bumped by accident. His was hard and unyielding, but warm. Very warm. He smelled good, too.

"Reardon, how about another towel?" Josh demanded, feeling Rebel shiver. "And, Tracy, how about finding some dry clothes for Ms. McCade?"

"Okay, okay." Tracy made a face as she stepped over the now-sleeping dog.

"What's his name?" Reardon asked, making a similar face as he backed out of the storage closet with another towel.

"Yellow Dog."

"What?"

Rebel laughed. A warm sound, Josh noted, as sassy and sexy as her smile. "Yeah. I know. Pretty dumb. My little brother named him."

She was taking off her slicker as she spoke, revealing that she was small and slim, almost fragile-looking, underneath. No wonder he had mistaken her for a boy. Except that there was nothing boyish or fragile about her slim, athletic body. The damp T-shirt she wore clung to her sexy curves like a second skin. Josh realized that Reardon, the imbecile, was flat-out staring.

At least Rebel didn't seem to notice. Didn't seem at all self-conscious about taking the towel from Reardon and drying her short-cropped hair right in front of them. Tousled, perky, she lifted her head and grinned.

"So. You guys ready to go to Marathon or not?"

Wonderful, Rebel thought. Absolutely perfect, in fact. A roomy main cabin, a working heater, a pot of creamy soup on the stove, a splash of wine poured by Reardon into a delicate crystal glass.

Rebel wasn't used to wine. Or the buttery soft cashmere sweater Tracy Tate had lent her. With its short, capped sleeves and deep jewel neckline, it seemed softer than the rose petals that shared the same color. The white silk capri pants were soft, too, though a little baggy at the cuffs since Tracy was taller than Rebel.

She'd had a good laugh while studying herself in the cabin mirror. *Resort wear* she'd always called these clothes. Strictly for the cruise-ship bunch.

But, man, they felt good. Sinful.

So did the wine that slid down her throat. It eased the chill from her bones. Brightened her eyes. She sat curled on the plump bench cushions while the wind gusted outside and the sailboat—the *Arabesque* as she'd been christened—creaked and rolled with the tide.

The squall had worsened during the past half hour. Tracy had withdrawn to one of the cabins, a little pale, a little wobbly on her feet. Apparently she wasn't much of a sailor. At the time Rebel had been talking with Pop on the radio, a crackly, static-filled conversation that had nonetheless reassured each of them that the other was okay.

Afterward she'd fixed the electrical short with Josh's help. Now the *Arabesque* was under way, and Josh had sent his cousin back to the helm, ignoring his complaints about the awful weather. The skiff was fastened by a tow cable to the stern. Yellow Dog had lapped up a bowl of soup and lay sleeping on the mat. Rebel sighed deeply. Who could possibly ask for more?

"So what were you doing all alone out on the ocean?"

She smiled at Josh's question. Her smile was dreamy from the wine. Or maybe because she wasn't used to such luxury. Or a man like him. She liked the way his chestnut hair lay thick and curly around his ears and nape. Liked the way his muscles bulged in the tight navy sweatshirt when he propped his arm along the back of the bench as he sat down across from her.

"I was fishing."

His brows shot up. "So far offshore?"

"Best place to fish."

"But in a boat like yours? With the weather so bad?"

She shrugged. He guessed she was used to being around boats, being by herself on stormy water. He remembered that she'd repaired the *Arabesque*'s wiring with little more than a pair of pliers. Squatting at the control panel with Tracy's capri pants hiked over slim brown calves, she looked adorable. Cute little butt, too. He'd had to send Reardon topside to keep him from staring.

"Yellow Dog," he said, changing the subject. "What exactly is he?"

The dog opened one round black eye at the sound of his name.

"Great Dane, Saint Bernard and labrador all mixed together."

"He's certainly...unusual."

"Thanks. I think."

They smiled at each other.

Suddenly she wanted to know all about him. Where he was from. Why he was sailing to Miami with his thoroughly inept sailor of a cousin. If he was married. But she was much too shy to ask the questions.

It had to be the wine.

She stole a glance at Josh's left hand. No ring.

"How about some more wine?" he asked.

She looked up to find him hovering close, the bottle in his hand. How could she refuse, with those dark eyes resting upon her, that granite chin only inches away?

"Sure."

She drank it much too fast and had to hide a very rude burp behind her hand. Grinning at him apologetically she found the courage to ask, "Do you have a last name?"

He started. "What? Oh, sorry. I guess I never introduced myself. It's Alden. Josh Alden."

A distant school memory stirred. "Like the pilgrim, John Alden?"

"As a matter of fact, yes. The same."

Rebel wasn't completely ignorant about the world beyond the Keys. A *Mayflower* descendant. That meant old, monied New England. It explained his presence aboard a sailboat like the *Arabesque*, the fine gold watch on his tanned wrist, the expensive loafers he wore.

But not why he was giving his kindly attention to someone like Rebel.

"Know what I think?" she ventured.

He smiled at her. God, he was cute when he smiled. Did he know that his eyes crinkled at the corners when he did? That a dimple appeared at the corner of his mouth? "No. What?"

"I think—"

But Rebel's words were drowned out by a violent jerk from the port side of the boat that nearly threw them to the deck. A loud ripping sound came from somewhere near the bow. In the cabin Tracy screamed. Yellow Dog was up and barking.

"What was that?" Josh demanded, leaping to his feet.

Rebel was already heading for the hatch. "I'm not sure, but if my guess is right you probably don't want to know."

"What's that supposed to mean?" he grated, following her.

"Unless I'm wrong, we just ran aground."

Chapter Two

"This is ridiculous! I can't believe this is happening! Oh, why didn't I fly to Nassau with Daddy? Momma tried to warn me. Do you remember, Reardon? She said—"

Rebel shook her head, ignoring the rest of Tracy's tirade. With Yellow Dog following at her heels she climbed to the deck again.

Josh was standing in the darkness near the aft rail. He glared at her when she appeared at his shoulder.

"What, you, too?" Rebel demanded with an exaggerated groan. "Just great. What am I supposed to do with you guys? I wish you'd believe me when I say it's not that bad. At least the radio on my boat still works. My father's coming to fetch us in the morning. We're not taking in water, right? So why is everybody so mad?''

Why? What was the matter with her? Josh wondered incredulously. Thanks to Reardon's stupidity, not to mention his gross inexperience and inattention, the *Arabesque* had drifted too far toward shore, hit a shoal, damaged her hull and shorted out her electrical system once again. All of it this time. No lights, no heater, no hot water. Nothing. And no prospect of being towed away until daylight.

"Look, I feel bad about the boat." Rebel's hand was on his arm. He wasn't too disgruntled to notice that her touch was light, warm. "Sure, it needs repairs. But the rain's stopped, and so has the wind. It's beautiful out here. Just look.''

He followed her pointing finger and saw stars pulsing in the clearing sky. Saw the pinpoint glitter of phosphorescence spangling the water. Smelled the tropical scent of salt and sea life. Of her. She was standing so close that he caught the fresh scent of sunshine, the outdoors, in her hair. It was much sweeter than any perfume.

He realized all at once that she was a lot shorter than he was. Looking down at her, he saw only the dark, tousled top of her head. "I guess we're making too big a deal out of this," he conceded reluctantly.

"Good. You're finally coming to your senses."

No, he wasn't. He'd agreed to take time off from

work to accompany his cousins from Tampa to Miami by boat, and now they were all but stranded on some unknown shoal in the Florida Keys. Tracy and Reardon were ready to murder each other, the main cabin had been taken over by a monstrous yellow dog and here he was letting a sassy castaway talk him out of being angry and making him think stupid thoughts about the way she smelled. No, he wasn't being the least bit sensible, in his opinion.

"You're still mad, aren't you?"

"You're too observant." And she was. Those wide blue eyes of hers missed nothing.

"Not exactly your idea of a vacation, huh?"

He looked at her again. Despite his temper he could feel a smile tugging at the corners of his mouth. Rebel McCade's constant cheeriness was too darned catching. He couldn't remember smiling this much to save his life.

"Not really, no."

"Then let's do something about it."

"Like what?" He'd never noticed before that her eyes sparkled every time she smiled.

"Well, we could pass the time a lot more pleasantly. Try to forget we're stuck here for the night."

He folded his arms across his chest. "Oh? Just how do you propose to do that?"

A wolfish grin, not at all sweet anymore, curved her lips. "Poker. Got any cards?"

* * *

By midnight she'd collected sixteen dollars from him and nearly twice that amount from Reardon. Now Reardon was sitting with his head buried in his hands, groaning, while Rebel counted her latest winnings.

She was all but gloating, Josh noticed. He had to turn his head to hide his smile. Straight-faced, he reached for the cards. "Who's ready for the next hand?"

As he spoke, the lantern they'd hung overhead began to sputter.

"Looks like we're running out of fuel," Reardon said. He sounded hopeful.

Rebel stood, yawning and stretching. "I guess that's it for me, then." Her dancing eyes met Josh's. "Where do you want me to sleep?"

Without warning he was struck by a vivid image of the two of them sharing his narrow bunk, their naked limbs entwined. He wondered if that trim little body of hers would be sleek or soft to the touch. Or both.

Thrown off balance, he couldn't answer right away.

Reardon did. He rose to his feet, scrubbing his hands across his face. "You can sleep with Tracy. She's got the biggest cabin."

Rebel remembered the retching sounds that had come from that cabin earlier. "Um. Do you mind if I bunk out here? Yellow Dog goes where I do, and I don't think she'd appreciate his company."

"No problem." Sliding out of the booth Reardon went to fetch a blanket.

Josh gathered up the cards. "Sure you'll be comfortable here?"

Rebel looked surprised. "Why not?"

"The bench is kind of narrow."

"No, I'll be fine. Really. I appreciate all of you taking me in like this."

"Don't forget that if we hadn't run aground you'd be home by now."

"Probably. But where's the fun in that?"

He thought about her words as he undressed in the aft cabin he shared with Reardon. So she considered this an adventure, did she? Well, that was her opinion. He himself had never been more annoyed or inconvenienced.

That's what being impulsive gets you, he thought dourly. If he hadn't agreed to Reardon's madcap plan, he wouldn't be stranded in pitch darkness on some unknown reef right now, sharing the limited space on board the *Arabesque* with a mutant yellow dog and his oddly named mistress, who was at present their sole hope of getting back to civilization.

Stripping to his boxer shorts, Josh stretched out on the bunk and propped his arms behind his head. Rebel McCade. Scarlett Elizabeth McCade. An image of her pixie face rose unexpectedly before him. The name might be strange, but the woman it belonged to certainly wasn't. A beauty—all eyes and pointed chin, and a luscious mouth that compelled a man to take a closer look whenever she was near.

What had Reardon said about her after she'd fixed their electrical system? *Best thing that's happened to us all day.*

Josh grinned, wondering if his cousin still felt that way now, after forking over thirty-five bucks to her at poker. Though well-heeled, Reardon was obsessively attached to his money.

As for Rebel McCade, she didn't seem to have too much of the stuff herself. Most working folk in the Keys probably didn't. At least, Josh assumed that Rebel worked. All he really knew about her was that her father owned a boat big enough to tow them home come morning. That, and the fact that the image of her wide blue eyes and smiling mouth still hovered stubbornly before him.

Rolling onto his side, Josh thrust the image away. He wasn't used to dwelling on women's faces, no matter how intriguing. And he wasn't interested in learning anything more about Rebel McCade. She was going to get them out of here come morning and that was all he needed to know.

"Mornin' everybody! Breakfast's ready!"

Josh stirred without opening his eyes. Reardon groaned, loud and long.

"Mr. Alden? Mr. Tate? How about some grub?"

"Who the devil is that?" Reardon demanded grumpily.

"Me, remember?"

Both men lifted their heads, blinking and disoriented.

"Over here, guys." Rebel was standing in the cabin door, hands on her hips, grinning saucily.

Josh rose on one elbow. Sunlight was pouring through the porthole. Crazy, but it didn't seem to match the warmth of Rebel's smile. He remembered hearing something about breakfast. Clearing his throat, he asked, "What's on the menu?"

"Fried mangrove snapper, roasted bananas, biscuits and honey. Oh, and a big pot of black coffee."

"I beg your pardon?" Now Reardon was staring at her, too.

"You heard me." She nudged his blanket with the toe of her sneaker. "Time to get up. I can't keep it warmed on the fire forever, and Pop'll be here soon."

Fire?

Josh came off the bunk like a scalded cat. Never mind that he was wearing nothing but his boxers. Never mind that this was the first time he'd actually seen Rebel McCade blush—and couldn't stand around to enjoy it. He was already scrambling into his clothes. "Where in hell did you build a fire?"

"Up on the deck."

Now it was Reardon who shot to his feet. "On my dad's boat?"

Rebel rolled her eyes. "Man, you guys are something! Think I'm really that dumb?"

Josh had to admit to a certain sheepishness when he followed her topside. They hadn't realized as much in the dark last night, but they'd run aground no more than a stone's throw from an uninhabited little key. The tide was out and Rebel must have waded ashore earlier. A driftwood fire crackled on the tiny shelf of a beach. Yellow Dog stood ankle deep in the water, tail wagging madly as he barked at their stranded boat.

"I can't believe this," Reardon said from behind them. "It's just like 'Gilligan's Island'." He turned appreciative eyes on Rebel. "Well, Ginger? Or is it Marianne? What was that about breakfast?"

"Better wake Tracy," Josh said curtly. What the devil was the matter with Reardon? He'd never known his cousin to act so goofy before. Was this his idea of flirting with a Florida native? Heaven help them all.

Rebel splashed nimbly into the thigh-deep water. "I'll serve up the grub in the meantime." She looked at Josh. "Are you coming?"

"Might as well."

"Watch out for the—"

As he dropped into the water his loafers sank completely into the sticky, sucking mud.

"—marl," she finished.

"What in hell is this stuff?" He could barely move. His feet were buried to the ankles and every time he tried to break free he lost one of his shoes. "Feels like quicksand."

"It's marl. Our ocean bottom. Just move slowly. You'll get used to it."

"Not if I can help it."

They started slogging toward shore. Rebel cast him an amused glance. "I know what you're thinking."

"Oh?" He didn't even bother hiding his irritation. "What's that?"

"You're thinking that the sooner you get out of here, the better."

He regarded her grumpily. "You happen to be right." Scowling, he took another look at her. "Don't tell me you still consider this to be an adventure?"

"Sure!" Her blue eyes were totally innocent. "Don't tell me you've got something better to do?"

He did. Plenty. Not knowing what was going on at the office, being without a fax or a phone, was not his idea of a restful time. In fact, it was starting to drive him crazy. Far better to be present at work than worrying about every little aspect of it from more than a thousand miles away.

The water was getting shallower, the bottom sandy, easier to navigate. Yellow Dog waded out to meet them, barking joyously. Ahead of them the water lapped against the shore. Palm fronds rustled in the breeze. Smoke from Rebel's cooking fire curled lazily.

The aroma of fresh-brewed coffee lifted some of

Josh's morning fog. His foul mood eased. "I guess we owe you an apology."

"For what?"

"The fire thing."

"Nah. You Yankees are just too easy to tease."

Josh was surprised to feel a grin coming on. "I'm not sure if I should take offense at that or not." In fact, he wasn't sure about anything where Scarlett Elizabeth McCade was concerned. He truly wasn't used to such an open, breezy woman. One who said exactly what she thought and didn't play by the usual rules. Or even seemed aware of them. Who woke up in the morning in such a cheerful mood.

To be fair, this wasn't even a remotely typical situation for him. Most women of Josh's acquaintance were encountered in crowded boardrooms or at high-impact meetings. Occasionally they were met, and sometimes pursued, at formal cocktail parties or lavish dinners. Not once in recent memory had one of them been thrust on him in the middle of a shipwreck. Small wonder he felt a little out of his depth where Rebel McCade was concerned!

"Most of the stuff in the fridge was already going bad," Rebel was telling him, "so I had to improvise." Kicking off her wet sneakers, she knelt to pour coffee. Ashes from the fire left a sooty streak on the thigh of her white capri pants. Tracy was going to have a fit, Josh thought.

"Here." She straightened and handed him the mug.

He cut his eyes away from those nimble legs of hers. "Thanks."

Their fingers touched when he took the mug from her. Rebel wasn't prepared for the spark that crackled between them. A slow, pleasurable humming seemed to start up in her head.

So, he was still doing it to her. Making her feel all strange and shivery inside, the way he had last night. Only this time she couldn't blame the wine.

She turned back to the fire, her movements unhurried. She didn't want Josh to know that she'd felt something leap between them. She kept her voice calm, too. "Hope you don't mind fish for breakfast."

"Better than nothing." Josh accepted the plate she fixed for him, being very careful this time not to let their fingers touch again. He didn't want her to know that he'd felt something strange happen the last time they did. Whistling for extra effect, he settled himself on a palm log. The air was warm. A faint breeze ruffled his dark curls. He shook his head.

"Amazing."

"What?"

"The fact that you actually went to the trouble of carrying dishes ashore." And the coffeepot and silverware, the honey and sugar. How had she managed without waking them up?

Rebel gave him an arch look. "We may be

stranded, Mr. Alden, but that doesn't mean we're going to eat like savages.''

"I see." He turned over the fish on the plate with his fork. Moist and flaky under some kind of breading, it smelled heavenly, but he still wasn't sure about seafood for breakfast.

"Where'd you get this?''

"Caught it fresh this morning.''

"Really? Where?''

Laughing, she gestured toward the ocean. "Out there. Where else?''

"Hey, I'm just an ignorant Yankee, remember?'' Josh took a hesitant bite. His eyes widened. She'd rolled the filets in flaked coconut—there'd been an unopened bag in the *Arabesque*'s pantry, he recalled—then panfried them over the fire with drizzled butter and honey on top. He'd never tasted anything so good.

"Do you like it?'' Rebel was studying him intently, a frown between her eyes.

"I can't believe it,'' he managed to say as he continued chewing.

"Does that mean it's good?''

"You bet.''

Relaxing, Rebel leaned forward without thinking and brushed a piece of coconut from the corner of his mouth. A fiery blush crept to her cheeks when she realized what she'd done. "Forgot the napkins. Sorry.''

"Don't be. This is perfect.'' He licked his lips.

Startled, he tasted her where she'd fleetingly touched him. He waited a moment before speaking again. "So, can I ask you a question?"

"What?"

"Where'd you learn to cook like this?"

She shrugged. Josh noticed that she had narrow, sloping shoulders that looked very slim and very sexy in her cropped cashmere top. "I taught myself. Sort of by necessity. My dad's an awful cook."

"What does he do?"

"Runs a fish camp on Gasparilla Key."

"A fish camp? What exactly is that?"

"We run fishing charters. Deep sea, backcountry, reefs or wrecks, light tackle, fly, any kind of fishing people want to do."

"Where does the camp part come in?"

"We've got a few cabins, a dining porch up at the house, rental boats, stuff like that."

"I see." But he couldn't exactly picture what a fish camp was supposed to look like. "And you cook for the guests?"

"Every night. Breakfast, too, if they want it."

Josh saluted her with his fork. "Lucky them."

Good, he thought. That put the whole damn thing neatly into perspective. Rebel McCade wasn't his type. In fact, the two of them were worlds apart. Just knowing that they were made it much easier for him to ignore all the inappropriate thoughts that had flashed through his head ever since he'd met her.

Rebel shaded her eyes. "Here come your cousins. You suppose we should warn them about the marl?"

"I don't know. Should we?"

They grinned wickedly at each other, then watched as Reardon, in shorts and a windbreaker, let himself down into the water and emitted a roar as he sank to his knees. Tracy, following him, screeched wildly.

Josh stood and cupped his hands. "Don't worry! It's not going to swallow you!"

"Thanks for telling us!" Reardon yelled back.

Tracy squealed as she took a step. "Eeewww! I hate this! Hate this, hate this, hate this!"

Josh settled back and gave Rebel an easy smile. "They're not used to roughing it."

Roughing it? Rebel couldn't help laughing. If this was roughing it, she'd died and gone to heaven. "Maybe they should have had their daddy's boat trailered to Miami."

"Definitely. I think Reardon's been reading too many yachting magazines."

"That's not where he learned to sail, is it? From magazines?"

"No. He flew to Tampa a week early to take some kind of course." Josh grinned sheepishly. "I don't think he paid much attention."

"Is that why you came along? To help him out?"

"Hardly. I'm not much of a sailor myself."

"So I've noticed."

He had to laugh at that. She was so refreshingly honest. "Actually, Reardon taunted me into coming. I should have ignored him."

I'm glad you didn't, Rebel thought.

"Oh, no!" That was Tracy, reaching shore. "My shoes are ruined!"

Yellow Dog danced around her, barking.

"Come have breakfast," Rebel called, whistling her dog to heel.

Tracy wouldn't touch the fish, but Reardon ate everything. When he'd polished off the last of the biscuits and wiped the crumbs from his shirt, he refilled his coffee mug and settled himself in the sand next to Rebel. His thigh brushed hers as he did so, but he made no attempt to scoot away.

Josh, watching them, felt a reaction in the pit of his stomach. Scowling, he refilled his own mug, telling himself he wasn't jealous. To prove as much, he leaned back to admire the view as though Reardon and Rebel didn't exist.

"So, how'd you get the name Rebel?" he heard his cousin ask. From the corner of his eye he could see the flash of that devilish Tate smile.

"My teachers at school. I didn't always exhibit model behavior."

"Ah, a disciplinary thing. Were you really that bad?"

"Unquestionably."

"I find that hard to believe."

Josh stared stubbornly out to sea even though he

could picture the smile deepening on Reardon's face. He was a handsome fellow, all right, and Josh had seen him use that boyish charm on a lot of women.

Not that he cared. He was just in the throes of a foul morning fog.

"Were you born here, Rebel?" Tracy asked, startling Josh. She didn't usually bother showing interest in other women. "Don't most people living in Florida come from somewhere else?"

"Not me. I was born in Marathon." Rebel sounded proud of it. "My dad's from Key Largo. Only, folks called it Rock Harbor back then."

"That's right." Tracy perked up. "They changed the name because of the movie. Funny part is, Bogie and Bacall never actually set foot there. The whole thing was filmed on a Hollywood sound stage." Josh had forgotten that she was a film buff.

"Pretty good," said Rebel. "Not many people know that."

"Thanks." Tracy was actually warming to her. Josh shook his head, surprised. The Tate women were usually extremely tough on the other members of their sex.

"*I* knew that." Apparently Reardon wasn't willing to share the spotlight with his sister.

Tracy tossed her head. "You did not."

"I did, too."

"Did not."

"Did."

For well-educated twenty-somethings they could act extremely infantile at times. Josh slapped the sand from his lap and rose to his feet. He'd had more than enough of them. "If you're done with breakfast, Reardon, maybe we'd better take a look at that hull."

Not that he knew much about it himself. But his cousin could use the exercise and save his fabled Tate charm for somebody else.

"Hey, look! Isn't that a boat?"

Everyone followed Tracy's pointing finger. Sure enough, a small black dot was speeding toward them across the green water. Sunlight glinted on glass. A frothy wake churned behind the stern.

Rebel bounced to her feet. "It's Pop! Time to clean up! Did everybody have enough to eat?"

Reardon nodded gravely. "Yes, thank you. Absolutely delicious. Unbelievable."

No doubt about it. He was laying it on with a trowel, Josh thought.

"In fact, let me give you a hand."

Josh watched, brows raised, as Reardon did the unthinkable: stacked together the dishes and tossed the leftovers to Yellow Dog.

That wasn't all. Now even Tracy was gaping as her brother actually got down on his hands and knees to shovel sand on the dying fire.

Well, well, well, Josh thought. Things were definitely getting interesting.

Chapter Three

Captain Robert "Pop" McCade was as small, wiry and tough as his daughter. Wind honed, leathery, with brilliant blue eyes and a thatch of unruly graying hair, he had the *Arabesque* readied for towing in a matter of minutes. He didn't say much as he worked. An unlit cigar stayed clamped between his teeth.

Rebel seemed to know what he wanted her to do without being told. They made quite a team, Josh noticed. While unraveling the line with nimble fingers, she told her father about yesterday's offshore fishing. About the snapper she had caught and fixed for breakfast. While tossing him the neatly knotted rope when he gestured for it, she described the Tates' first encounter with marl.

"Wonder how come I never say a word?" Pop McCade's twinkling blue eyes met Josh's. The two men were thigh deep in water, righting the sailboat with the help of the cable and the tide. "Never can get one o' my own in edgewise."

"I heard that, Pop."

Rebel and Yellow Dog were in the stern of the McCade boat, a cabin cruiser that had the look of many hard years on her. She didn't even have a name. Reardon had asked about that when Pop had helped him on board.

"Backcountry boats don't need names," he'd said with a snort.

Reardon had taken Pop's answer as an insult to his intelligence, although Pop hadn't meant it that way. He just didn't know Pop, Rebel thought. Still, sufficiently cowed, Reardon had withdrawn with Tracy to the bow of the boat to watch the proceedings.

"Don't need his help," Pop had said when Josh started to wave his cousin back. He'd obviously sized up both men and put his faith in Josh. "Now we're gonna ease 'er out slow. Hope she comes clear without much fuss. Reb!" Pop shouted across to her. "Start the engine! Keep the line taut till I get there!"

Yellow Dog greeted them at the ladder, slobbering and whining. Pop slapped him good-naturedly with his baseball cap. Taking over the wheel he throttled back gently, then set the boat heading forward.

Rebel whooped when the *Arabesque* righted herself and slipped into place behind the stern. Tracy and Reardon applauded.

They made quite a convoy with both the sailboat and Rebel's little skiff bobbing in their wake.

"There's sandwiches in the cooler," Pop informed them once they were out in the channel. "Gonna take a while to get home." He grinned at Rebel. "Nothin' fancy like yours. Peanut butter and jelly."

"Sounds good to me." Reardon rummaged enthusiastically through the cooler.

"Where'd you find these guys?" Pop asked Rebel over the stuttering of the engine.

"I told you. Conch Shoals."

"What do they do?"

"I've no idea."

"Think they might like to do some fishing?"

"Pop, put your greedy mitts behind your back. They're not interested."

"Even that one?" He nodded toward Josh, who stood at the stern keeping an eye on the tow line.

Rebel used his question as an excuse to look at Josh herself. No doubt about it, she liked looking at him. He was certainly easy on the eye. Much better than his fussy, well-groomed cousin.

"No."

There was a surprising tremor around her heart

as she realized she'd be saying goodbye to Josh at the Marathon marina.

"You sure? He looks like the type who'd enjoy some bluewater fishin'. Those biceps—"

"Pop. Forget it."

"We got a weekend tournament coming up."

"I said forget it."

"I could use a new outboard if we win the—"

Rebel reached over to clamp his mouth shut.

There were hoots and catcalls from the docks lining the big commercial marina at Marathon when the McCades finally puttered in.

"Hey, Pop! Ain't that boat a bit over the limit? You shoulda throwed it back!"

"New way to bring in clients, McCade? Bumping holes in their hulls?"

"Really gettin' desperate, ain't he?"

"Jackasses," Pop muttered around his cigar.

Rebel jumped onto the dock and helped ease the sailboat in without knocking the damaged hull against the pilings. She made fast the ropes while Pop cut the engine.

Josh appeared at her elbow. "Need help?"

"Here." She handed him one of the lines and watched him secure it to the dock cleats. She noticed he wasn't as inexperienced as he'd said.

Reardon climbed clumsily from the bow. "We really appreciate this, Mr. McCade."

"Cap'n McCade. But you can call me Pop. Everybody does."

"Thank you, sir." Reardon didn't sound too enthusiastic.

He probably doesn't think much of Pop, Rebel thought. Usually Pop didn't care enough to give people the time of day—unless they had money. Then he was all over them, sweet-talking them into a fishing excursion or a snorkeling trip. Yes, sir, Pop being pleasant to the likes of Reardon Tate was really something to see.

"Come on." Pop stepped down onto the dock. "I'll introduce you fellows to a mechanic."

While they were gone, Rebel busied herself stowing gear. A few of the locals came over to inquire about the crippled sailboat. Rebel knew perfectly well that most of them just wanted to get a closer look at Tracy Tate. She was certainly something to look at wearing skimpy shorts and a bathing suit top while sunning herself against the cabin wall. Unlike most northern visitors she already had a golden tan. She'd probably started working on it even before the *Arabesque* left Tampa.

Unfortunately for her admirers, Tracy made it clear that she wasn't interested. She didn't have to say an actual word. One chilly look was enough to send every interested male slinking back to his boat. Rebel, rinsing off her fishing gear, kept her head bowed so that none of them would see her grinning.

Pop came back a few minutes later tailed by

Reardon Tate. Reardon didn't look very happy. Or becoming, to be perfectly honest. His nose was sunburned and his shorts were crusted with salt. His forearms were the hue of cooked lobster.

"Yecch," said Tracy, opening her eyes. "You are going to peel something awful, big brother."

"Don't I know it."

"Well, at least you have an excuse. It isn't every day we're marooned. Where's Josh?"

"Filling out paperwork. I've been on the phone with Dad. Trace, the boat's going to need repairs."

"D-uh. How long will it take?"

"Probably a week."

Tracy shot upright. "A week! A week in this place? Reardon, have you gone nuts?"

"Calm down, will you? We're not going to stay. Dad said we should go on to Miami. Catch a flight from there and meet him in Nassau. He'll send for the boat later."

"What about Josh?" Tracy asked, echoing Rebel's thoughts. "Is he flying straight home from Miami?"

"Actually, he's going to stay here with the boat."

"What!"

"Well, somebody has to! You'd rather it was us?"

Tracy looked around the crowded marina with its dilapidated bait shop, the buckets of chum stored at the edge of the dock, the scruffy locals hanging about. She shivered. "No thanks."

"Well." Reardon looked satisfied. "Josh said he didn't mind. I've rented a car. They'll be bringing it around any minute. We'd better get our stuff."

He disappeared down the *Arabesque*'s hatch as he spoke. Rebel, who hadn't said a word during their exchange, resumed rinsing her equipment with the marina hose.

Pop came over and stood with his arms folded across his chest, watching her. "What're you smiling at?"

"I'm not smiling."

"And is that a hum I hear? I could swear I hear you hummin'."

"I'm not. I never hum."

But she was. And the sound was echoing pleasantly in her head. Gasparilla Key, the tiny island the McCades called home, lay just across the channel on the bay side of Marathon. Because there weren't any stores or roads or groceries there, everything had to be purchased here in town. Rebel usually made the trip over by boat once or twice a day. Surely that meant there was a chance she'd run into Josh Alden during the week that he'd be staying here. Maybe, just maybe, she'd have the nerve to invite him to dinner one night.

Tracy appeared on deck with a bulging designer tote over one shoulder. Pop gallantly helped her onto the pier.

"Did Josh have any idea where he was going to stay?" she asked him.

Rebel's heart plummeted at the question. She'd forgotten that a midwinter sailfish tournament started tomorrow. Josh was going to have a hard time finding a room, especially here in Marathon. No doubt he'd end up staying at one of the larger resorts on Long Key, which usually had vacancies. That meant she'd have no chance at all of running into him.

"We phoned around a bit." Pop took the cigar out of his mouth long enough to smirk at his daughter. "Wasn't nothin' to be had for miles. Not this time of year. That's why I invited him to stay with us."

Rebel's head came up with a jerk. "You did what?"

"Invited him to stay. You know we got that one empty cabin now that—"

"Pop! How could you!"

He blinked, feigning surprise. "Now, honey, I was only bein' neighborly."

"Neighborly!" Rebel waited until Tracy had moved out of earshot, then dropped her voice to a hiss. "You're taking advantage of him is what you're doing! You've always been able to smell money a mile away, and now you can't wait to sink your hooks into Josh Alden! Well, listen here. I'm not going to let you fleece him by talking him into entering that tournament, or renting him our most expensive boat or—"

"Reb, Rebel, honey." Pop was holding up his hands, looking as wounded as Yellow Dog when he was passed over for table scraps. "What kind of word is that? *Fleece* him? You make me sound like a dishonest, rascally—"

"Pop, I *know* you. You've got dishonest and rascally down to an art. So I have every right to—"

"Besides, I don't intend to do any such thing," he was saying as though she hadn't spoken. "You told me yourself he's not a fisherman, right? So I'll just leave him alone. At least this way we got us a full house for the week and he's got himself a nice place to stay till his boat's fixed."

Rebel's mouth thinned. "I still don't trust you."

"I know you don't. And it breaks my paternal heart into half a million pieces."

Rebel's response was a loud snort. She knew Pop far too well to consider Josh—and his wallet—safe from his clutches. And much as she loved her home on Gasparilla Key, she didn't think Josh would be comfortable there. He'd be better off at one of those luxury resorts on Duck Key or up at Islamorada. A place with room service. A heated pool. Endless stacks of plush towels.

For the first time in her life Rebel felt a twinge of embarrassment as she envisioned her home. As though her conscience was forcing her to admit that it wasn't good enough, fancy enough, for Josh.

And boy, that infuriated her. As did Pop's unabashedly angelic expression.

"Okay," she said through her teeth. "We'll put him up in number four. I agree we could use the money after the Beckwiths had to cancel. But if you try to wrangle one thin dime out of him—"

"Whoa! I told you—"

Her chin jutted. Her eyes spit fire. "Just remember what I said."

"Okay, okay." He turned away, shaking his head. "Too much like her dadburned mother."

So this was the place Rebel called home: a weathered sign reading McCades' Fish Camp nailed to a piling at the broken-down dock. All sorts of fishing equipment scattered on the pier. Boats tied up willy-nilly near a palm-frond shack. A shell walk through twisted green jungle and the tiniest stretch of lawn, like a postage stamp, tumbling down to the bay. There was no beach. Just a drop-off, but at least it was clean of flotsam and coral. The water sparkled with golden sun coins.

Four little cottages with tumbledown, sagging shutters surrounded the lawn. Flowers were everywhere. In window boxes and on blooming vines that inched up and over the roof. Each cottage was a different timeworn color: pastel pink, periwinkle, mint and buttercream. The McCades' house was one-story, trimmed with peeling gingerbread, flanked on three sides by screen porches. It was old, sagging, but sort of charming, thanks again to the flowers crammed into every imaginable container on the steps, the porches and the crumbling terrace: lobster traps, old paint cans, even an oil drum.

Pop McCade pushed past Josh, who'd stopped on the path to stare. "Used to be a real workin' camp till my daughter got her hands on it."

"I heard that, Pop. All I did was have the junk hauled off."

"Perfectly good stuff, you mean. Stuff I wish I still had."

"Rotting timbers, Pop? Appliances that didn't work? Sheet-metal scraps?"

"Like I said. Important stuff I coulda used."

"You should've seen it when I got back from college," Rebel said in an undertone to Josh.

McCade turned to glare at her. "I heard that, missy."

Great. I'm in the middle of another family feud, Josh thought. He'd seen the poisonous looks father and daughter had been exchanging ever since they'd left Marathon. Never mind that they'd been steering two different boats: McCade in his big cruiser, Rebel and Yellow Dog in the flat-bottomed skiff.

Josh had sat on the cooler behind Pop, pretending not to notice. He'd had no idea what had set them off, but he certainly wasn't about to get involved.

"Come on. I'll show you where you're staying."

Rebel had taken a key ring down from the back

door of the house. Now she unlocked the mint green cottage and stepped aside to let Josh in.

"We had a cancellation yesterday. It doesn't happen often. I'll have the bed made up in a minute." She was opening the windows and tilting out the hurricane shutters as she spoke. "There's ice water in the fridge near the bathroom door. No bathtub, just a shower. Hope that's all right. There're two bedrooms, but the beds in each are kind of small. Sorry."

She looked him up and down as she spoke. It was hard to imagine a man of Josh's size being comfortable in a twin bed.

For some reason it wasn't hard at all to think of him in bed, though. Rebel could feel a wave of heat rushing to her cheeks. Quickly she whirled to open the linen cupboard.

"Fresh towels are in here. The sheets are up at the house. I'll bring them right over. There's a TV, but no phone. You can make calls in—"

"Rebel."

Her hands fell to her sides. "What?"

His lips were twitching. Lord, he was sexy when he smiled. "You don't have to be so worried. I like it."

Her eyes went wide. "Y-you do?"

He looked around him. Tongue-in-groove ceilings, beaded board walls that were whitewashed and clean. A braided rug on the floor. Old, mismatched furniture painted in the same, sunset colors as the cottages. "Why wouldn't I?"

She put her hands behind her back. Her expression reminded him of a small child caught in a lie. "I-I don't know."

But of course she did. That much was obvious to Josh. She'd expected him to be turned off by the lack of luxury, of fancy amenities, by the admitted shabbiness of the place. Did she think him as big a snob as Reardon?

Obviously.

For some reason, that hurt.

She was looking down at the tips of her sneakers. "I hope you won't be bored staying here a whole week. There isn't much to do."

"Your father said I could take one of the boats over to Marathon if I wanted to."

She nodded. "Some of our guests do that."

"Know what? I don't think I will."

Her head came up. She regarded him earnestly. "Oh?"

His dark eyes were intent on her face. He was smiling that devastating smile again. "You probably won't believe this, but I like the idea of having nothing to do."

"I suppose you need a vacation to recover from your vacation with Reardon, huh?"

He laughed. "You know, I think you may be right."

Strange, but at the moment he really meant it.

There was something about the Keys, about the pace of life, the sultry warmth and exotic ways, that made a person want to slow down. Made the frenzied world back home stop seeming so vitally important. As if he had suddenly been handed the assurance that his life wouldn't collapse into chaos just because he took a week off in this strange little place the McCades called home.

Josh shook his head to clear it. Who had planted such radical ideas in his mind? Rebel McCade? Not surprising, since she had to be the most radical departure from tradition, from familiarity, he'd ever encountered.

He wondered if she was aware that she was having this strange effect on him. He wondered if she knew that he was intrigued by her boundless energy and laughter, her short, sassy hair and big blue eyes, all of which was packaged so neatly in a compact, sexy body?

Rebel, watching Josh's rugged face soften unconsciously, had no inkling of his thoughts, but all at once an air of promise, like a present waiting to be opened, seemed to hover between them. She took a step backward, shaken by the force of her response to it. Alarm bells went off in her brain.

Oh, no, you don't, she thought. She'd been helping Pop run the fish camp long enough to admit that sometimes one of their guests turned out to be a man she found attractive, who seemed to find her attractive in turn. She'd made a point never to tease or flirt with any of them because she was dead set against doing anything unprofessional, anything that might jeopardize the reputation McCades' had established over the years. Besides, she wasn't the type to enter into casual affairs, period.

Oh, sure, she found Josh Alden attractive. Okay, very, very attractive, she admitted to herself. And he did funny things to her insides that she wasn't used to. But he was still a paying guest and she was going to start treating him like one.

Which ought to be pretty easy considering that she'd been working here long enough.

She took a deep breath and delivered the speech she'd made a thousand times before, to a thousand different people who had never once tied her stomach into knots: "Dinner's usually served around seven. Make sure you let me know every morning whether you're going to be here or not so I can set a place for you. Same thing holds for breakfast. Just let me know the night before what you'll be wanting. That's as far as it goes for rules around here. Oh, and if you need anything, anything at all, just ask at the house. We'll do our best to provide it."

She does that amazingly well, Josh thought. Slipped without effort into the role of innkeeper, letting him know with little more than a change in the tone of her voice, the way she held her head, that he was now her paying guest and that they would no longer be sharing the intimacy of being stranded on a disabled boat together.

Admittedly, it was easier to think of her in terms of a woman who worked the front desk of a fish camp than to dwell on the spark that had flared between them on more than one occasion since they'd met. He, too, knew better than to fan that spark into anything more. For a lot of sensible reasons.

Rebel McCade was not his type. Bluntly speaking, she was a fisherman's daughter.

His mother would be horrified.

His friends would think him deranged.

He was simply not going to pursue his interest in her any further. No matter how full and sweet her mouth. No matter how sexy her body. No matter that barely a minute ago he'd been fantasizing about Rebel in a way that had nothing to do with housekeeping.

He moved to the window and pushed the blinds aside, trying to think of something conversational that would help cement the distance between them. "How many guests do you have at the moment?"

"We've got four coming in tonight. I'm driving to Miami to pick them up."

"I thought your father told me you were booked."

"We are."

"Only four?"

"We never accept more than Pop's boat can hold at any one time. Six in the thirty-four footer, four in the twenty-five."

"But how can you make money with so few guests?" He was thinking about the shabbiness of the place. "Why don't you build more cottages? Take in more people? Not everyone wants to go after marlin or tuna or whatever. Why can't they just enjoy the scenery? That little beach out there?"

"Because we're a fish camp, Josh."

He turned his head to find her smiling at him. "What? Did I say something stupid?"

"We take in all the money we need with our charters. Trust me."

"How? This place isn't costing me much."

"That's because we don't charge a lot for the cottages. Pop's little black book is where the real money lies."

"Sorry, you lost me."

"That's where he keeps track of the best places to fish," Rebel explained patiently. "The location and depths of grouper holes, reef wrecks, things like that. It all depends on what his clients want." She was pulling the chenille spread off the bed as she spoke, her movements quick and practiced. "A good charter boat captain—and Pop is one of the best—can pretty much command whatever he wants."

Josh was interested despite himself. "Is that right?"

Rebel nodded. "People come from all over the country, even from Europe, to fish with him. Most of our guests are old-timers. They've spent the past ten, fifteen, even twenty years with us. The guys coming in tonight? I've known them since I was seven.''

Josh had to smile at the thought of Rebel at seven. She must have been adorable. A handful, too. The way she was now.

"So what do people do with the fish they catch?"

"Eat them, mostly. Not the trophy catches, of course. They get thrown back. South Florida has an aggressive tag and release program. I make sure Pop abides by the law.''

"Meaning he wouldn't if he could get away with it?"

Rebel grinned. "He should've been born two hundred years ago. That way he could've declared himself a pirate officially. Nowadays he just acts sneaky. Sometimes I think there isn't an honest bone in his body. Be careful around him, Josh. He'll empty your wallet before you realize it.''

"I'll consider myself forewarned.''

They smiled at each other, Rebel wistfully, Josh refusing to acknowledge a twinge of regret. Both of them knew they should be grateful for the ease with which they had slipped into the role of inn-keeper and guest.

But still.

"About dinner." Josh cleared his throat. "Do you mind if I take a raincheck tonight?"

Rebel shook her head. She wouldn't admit to feeling disappointed.

"I want to go to bed early. Catch up on sleep. We didn't have much once that storm blew up and Reardon got us lost."

She laid the folded bedspread neatly over a chair. "I'll have your bed made up right away, then. You can take a nap now, if you like. As for lunch, I can leave a tray outside your door."

"Won't Yellow Dog eat it?"

"He knows better." She pursed her lips, considering. "But the seagulls might."

"Then maybe we better skip that. Tell you what. I'll run into Marathon with one of your boats and grab a bite while you make up the room. Maybe I'll take a look around while I'm at it. That way you won't have to rush. What do you think? Is that all right?"

No, it wasn't. Not really. She hated the way they were talking so stiffly to each other, discussing something as depressing as housekeeping, avoiding each other's eyes. She'd made a mistake at the Marathon marina in thinking that having him here was going to be wonderful. She should have realized that their relationship would change the moment he signed his name to their register. But she smiled at him brightly, slanting her gaze up at his craggy, handsome face without a twinge of longing. Or so she hoped.

"That'll be fine. I'll have everything ready when you get back."

"Great. Could you show me which boat to use?"

"Gladly." Hurrying up to the house to fetch the keys, she decided that she was in for a miserable week.

Darn you, Pop, why on earth did you ask him to stay?

Chapter Four

An awful scream woke Josh from a sound sleep the following morning. Heart pounding, he threw open the shuttered door. Blinding sunlight greeted him. Once outside, the screams were deafening. He squinted as he looked around. What was going on?

"Will you shut up!" he heard Rebel yelling at the top of her lungs. As she turned the corner and saw him in the doorway, she smiled at him, instant sweetness and innocence. "Good morning. How did you sleep?"

"Fine, until now."

Fortunately for him the screaming had stopped with Rebel's shouted command. He ran a shaky hand through his curls. "What in the name of God was that?"

Rebel put down the laundry basket she'd been carrying." Pop's macaw. She hates it when he doesn't take her along."

"Where'd he go?"

"Fishing."

"By himself?"

"No. He's got charters all week, remember? I picked them up around six last night, after you'd gone to bed."

"I was tired," Josh said somewhat defensively.

"I know."

Bleary-eyed, he saw that she was twinkling at him. He'd forgotten that she was one of those endlessly cheerful morning people. Disgusting. "I need coffee," he grumped.

"There's some at the house. Come on up as soon as you're ready. Oh, and Josh—"

"Hmm?"

"The macaw's on the back porch. Please stay away from her. She bites."

"Believe me, there's no need to worry."

He quickly showered and shaved. Still foggy brained, he nicked himself more than once. The sunshine hurt his eyes as he crossed the shell walk to the back terrace of the main house. He couldn't even spare a glance at the sparkling green of the bay. What was that nonsense he'd been spouting yesterday about wanting a vacation?

Sure, he'd slept like a log. But the Keys were too quiet. The night was too dark. And he'd had dreams—nightmares, really—about what was going on at work without him. He'd have to call the office right away. Leave instructions, dictate strategies, organize his staff. No doubt they were taking full advantage of their boss's rare absence.

Vacation? He must have lost his mind.

Opening the screen door, he felt his eardrums vibrate beneath the onslaught of renewed screams. Rebel came bursting out of the house to toss a cover over the wrought-iron cage.

Josh shook his head, hoping to make the ringing stop. No dice. "Does she always scream like that?"

"Whenever she thinks she can get away with it." Rebel lifted a corner of the cover. "Well? Are you gonna behave? Want to come out?"

"Okay," came the hoarse response. "Be good, now."

"She can talk," Josh said, astonished.

"Regrettably."

The cover came off. The macaw was gorgeous, a deep scarlet red trimmed with yellow, green and blue. Beady, baleful eyes stared at Josh. He swore he could read icy disdain in them. Great. The bird hated him. They hadn't even been introduced.

"What's her name?"

"Monster."

That figured.

"Here. Have a seat. I'll fetch breakfast," Rebel said.

Josh poured himself a mug of coffee from the

thermos on the table. By the time Rebel returned he'd managed to down another one and was feeling decidedly more human. Enough to finally take an interest in his surroundings. The long, screened porch was cooled by numerous ceiling fans. Through the flowering shrubs outside he caught glimpses of brilliant green water. The air was warm. Soft. Very tropical. Behind him in the cage, Monster cracked seeds and muttered to herself.

Rebel was carrying a tray. In denim shorts and a white T-shirt she looked tanned and very fit. Very native. Very sexy. He remembered what he'd decided the night before and felt a pang of regret.

"I fixed some eggs, bacon and grits. There's toast in the basket, and jam on the table." She was unloading the tray in front of him as she spoke. "If you want more I'll be happy to—"

She broke off as Josh clamped a hand on her wrist. His big fingers closed around soft skin. She went still and looked at him questioningly.

"You made grits?"

She nodded.

"Uh, Rebel, I hate to say this—"

"Let me guess." Her lips curved. "You've never had 'em before."

"Nor do I intend to."

"You know them's fightin' words, don't you, Yankee?"

He let go of her wrist, then leaned back and studied her with lazy pleasure. She was something to look at all showered, clean and well-rested, with her dancing blue eyes, dark, cropped hair and sleek, golden skin. A warning bell was going off in his brain, but he paid no attention. How could he? Smiling and playful, Rebel was impossible to resist.

He leaned back even farther in his chair and crossed his hands behind his head. "Just how do folks fight around here, Ms. Scarlett Elizabeth McCade?"

"Ooh! Ain't nobody dares call me that!" she drawled in mock fury. Never mind that Florida wasn't really Southern. Talking like that, tilting her head coquettishly, she could have passed for a blue-blooded belle anywhere south of the Mason-Dixon line.

Josh cocked an eyebrow at her. "So what are you going to do about it?"

With astonishing speed she grabbed him in a headlock and had him facedown on the table with his arm behind his back before he even knew what hit him.

"I suppose you want me to say uncle now," he said, his voice muffled because he was speaking into the vinyl tablecloth.

"Heck, no. You're gonna eat those grits."

"No...I'm...not." His calm denial was interspersed with two short breaths as he easily and painlessly freed himself. Seconds later it was Rebel lying on the table, face up, with Josh leaning over her, his arms propped on either side of her head.

"Now it's your turn."

She giggled. "Okay, okay, I'll eat 'em."

"No, that's not what I had in mind."

"Uncle, then."

"Or that, either."

"What, then?"

"Stop wriggling."

But she wouldn't. And because he was leaning over her, effectively pinning her to the table with the lower half of his body, she was having a wildly arousing effect on him.

She must have sensed as much at exactly the same time, because all of a sudden he saw her pupils widen and her eyes grow dark. Her smile faded. She looked at him, silent now.

"Know what I want?" he persisted, leaning close.

"No," she breathed, her eyes drawn despite themselves to his mouth.

"I want you to kiss me."

"That—that's stupid!" But she didn't sound like her usual, cocky self.

"No arguing. Remember, to the victor belong the spoils."

"Okay, okay." Lifting her head from the table she gave him a quick, sisterly smack on the jaw.

"That was awful."

"Well, what did you expect?" she demanded, scowling.

He leaned closer until his mouth hovered a mere

inch above hers. "Something like this." He slowly lowered his head and gently brushed her lips. "Or this." His lips parted hers as their breaths mingled. "Or this." The kiss was incredibly slow, incredibly erotic. Especially when he increased the pressure, easing her lips even farther apart with his own.

"Oh," said Rebel. "Oh."

It was a slow-motion kiss. One that he let build like a subtle, incoming tide. His hands moved to cup her face. His body shifted. Easing himself closer, his hips found hers and locked there so that they touched, center to center.

Dazed, Rebel felt the slow heat of longing fan through her. Everywhere. A dreamy burn. She sighed and let her arms curl around his neck.

Acknowledging her surrender, Josh pressed closer, his tongue seducing hers. He'd been wanting to taste her full, luscious mouth from the moment he'd seen her.

Rebel's kiss was sweeter than he'd imagined. And much more dangerous. He could feel himself drowning in her womanly warmth. Already he was stirring, his body hardening insistently against her. Any moment now he'd be crossing that dangerous line where a kiss would no longer be enough.

So he eased himself back. Difficult as it was, much as he hated to. But he knew that he must.

Because he knew that if he kept on kissing her, he'd want more. Too much. He wasn't looking for a casual affair. Besides, Rebel McCade wasn't his type any more than he was hers. Not by a long shot.

"There. That wasn't so bad, was it?" He ended the kiss with an easy smile and a joke, wanting to let her know that he only *sounded* breathless, that his blood wasn't thrumming, that he was teasing her because he wanted to spare her any embarrassment.

He should have known better. The moment he stepped away, Rebel bounded to her feet. Grinning, she fluffed her fingers through her disheveled hair. "So. You gonna taste my grits or not, Yankee?"

What could he say? Sitting down, he pulled the bowl toward him and took a defiant bite. But he tasted only her. Found himself aching all over again for her.

"Not bad."

Surprisingly, he was telling the truth. Grits really weren't all that bad. At least not Rebel's. She'd stirred in cream, coarsely ground pepper, chunks of breakfast ham. The grits actually complemented the bacon and scrambled eggs.

"Told you." Rebel was relieved that her voice came out just fine while she stood at his shoulder watching him eat. She'd been scared to death she would end up sounding all shaky and short of breath. That her voice alone would tip him off to the fact that she wasn't feeling nearly as indifferent as she wanted him to think.

No, she wasn't indifferent, and who in heck

could blame her? She'd never been kissed like that to save her life, never been tossed down on a table and seduced with just the lazy pressure of a masculine mouth! Damn it, she was still humming inside, and there he sat shoveling breakfast into that same, sexy mouth of his and pouring himself another cup of coffee as though nothing had happened.

Fuming, she snatched up the tray and marched back inside.

Serves you right, Rebel McCade. You don't mess around with a man like that! Don't you know he's way, way out of your league?

Yes, he was, even though he was a lot more subtle about his wealth and privileged background than either of his cousins. He was well-mannered, too, considering that he'd gone out of his way to be kind and polite to Pop, and to her. Still, there was no mistaking that folks with names like Alden and Tate moved in far different circles than the McCades of Gasparilla Key.

Darn it, she'd better remember that. All the rest of this week. Every dadblasted minute!

Full of angry energy she washed the dishes, swept the kitchen, then went upstairs to make her brother's bed. Normally, Lee lived in Michigan with their mother, but he was on winter break from middle school. Since he was taking Rebel's place as deckhand on Pop's boat while he was here, he'd left with the rest of them at dawn.

When Rebel came back downstairs Yellow Dog was waiting for her in the hall. His pricked ears and wildly wagging tail let her know there was someone in the kitchen. Curious, she went to take a look.

It was Josh, of course. He was standing just inside the back door with his hands in his pockets, grinning rather sheepishly.

"Hope you don't mind that I let myself in. I need to use the phone."

Lord, that grin! Would she ever get used to it? At least she'd managed to get over his kiss. So much so, in fact, that she could grin right back at him as though it had never happened. If he could pretend, then so could she—even better.

"A phone? Sure." Her voice sounded totally unaffected and friendly. "There's one in the study. Come on, you'll have more privacy there."

"What about this one?" He gestured toward the portable unit on the counter.

"Help yourself." Whistling for added effect, she went outside with the dog. The screen door slammed behind her.

Josh's smile faded. He'd be damned if he'd let that woman get under his skin. Scowling, he dialed, waiting until a familiar male voice came on the line. "Hello, Walters."

"Mr. Alden! What a relief! We heard you'd been shipwrecked."

Shipwrecked! Josh put a hand to his brow. That must have been Reardon, ringing his mother from

Miami with dramatic embellishments concerning the gravity of their plight. Walters, loyal old butler that he was, hadn't been spared the gruesome details.

"No one was shipwrecked, Walters. Reardon's been hallucinating again."

"What a relief, sir."

"I would have called sooner had I known."

"We understand, sir. What did happen?"

"Nothing serious. Uncle Archer's new boat ran into some coral and now I'm here in—"

"Is that Josh?" He could hear his mother's anxious voice in the background. "Let me speak to him, please!"

"Very good, mada—"

Josh could almost envision the receiver being snatched from the long-suffering butler's outstretched hand. Then Helena Alden's lovely, lilting accents came down the wire.

"Darling! How are you?"

"Good morning, Mother. Fine, actually."

"Reardon called last night with the most dreadful news. I've been on pins and needles waiting for you to phone. Really, Josh, you might have thought of me a little."

"Sorry, Mother."

"My entire day was ruined. I wasn't able to do anything, go anywhere—"

Josh grinned.

"—and I haven't eaten a single bite since luncheon yesterday. Just ask Walters."

Unintelligible mumbling could be heard in the background.

"Yes, Walters, I'm aware of it. Now, go away and let me finish talking to Josh. Josh, dear, Reardon says you'll be staying in Florida another week. Is it true? Did you call Tony to let him know?"

"Of course I did." Tony Clarke was Josh's right-hand man in the Providence office of the family firm.

"Do you really intend to stay away that long?" Helena Alden sounded as disbelieving as Tony had.

Josh smothered a twinge of irritation. His refusal to take time off from work was a long-standing point of contention between him and his family. Nothing short of nuclear annihilation could keep Josh from the office, Reardon had always said.

An old joke, not funny any more.

"Mother, you know Uncle Archer. He'd want someone here overseeing repairs, and Reardon wasn't about to stay."

"Yes, I know. Tracy said the same thing. She thought the Keys dreadfully disappointing. Very shabby. Overcrowded. Tacky. She says you're staying at some sort of fish camp? Whatever is that? It doesn't sound very savory."

Josh turned to look out the kitchen window. Through the rustling palm fronds he could see the bay sparkling in the sunshine. He caught a glimpse

of his mint green cottage on the far side of the lawn.
"It's actually quite charming."

His mother made a rude noise. "Reardon says
you're mainly interested in the girl that runs the
place. A wild savage, he said. Do be wise. She
sounds terribly ordinary."

Josh closed his eyes for a moment. Right now he
wanted very much to punch his cousin Reardon in
the mouth. Mixed with the fury rising to his throat
was the grudging realization that he didn't really
have the right to be angry. Reardon, idiot though
he was, had somehow touched on something that
Josh had denied until now: that he'd accepted Pop
McCade's offer to stay on Gasparilla Key when he
could have gone anywhere else because of Rebel.
Because he'd been curious about her home. About
her.

Well, he'd found out more than he wanted to
know about Rebel thanks to the wild assault on his
senses he'd experienced while kissing her. Okay,
so maybe he was attracted to her, enough so that
even doltish Reardon Tate had noticed. Then again,
Reardon hadn't exactly been impervious to her himself.

"Look, Mother, there's really no need to worry."
Not about a fisherman's daughter...
"I'm quite capable of looking after myself."
"Oh, yes, I'm well aware of that." His mother
actually chuckled. "Dear, predictable Josh."
Now why did he feel annoyed at that? Gritting

his teeth, he gave her the number where he was staying and promised to let her know the moment he'd booked a flight home. He assured her again that there was no cause for worry because he was truly capable of looking after himself.

"I know," she repeated. "I only hope you won't be too miserable in that…that place. Are the rooms sanitary? The baths scrubbed? Linens clean?"

"Mother—"

"Oh, all right." She laughed, again without rancor. "Good luck, my darling. From what Reardon said you'll be needing it."

He hung up without sharing her amusement. Feeling annoyed with her and not really knowing why.

"Coffee," he said aloud. He needed one more mug to soothe his morning irritation, that was all.

Around lunchtime he borrowed one of the camp's boats and puttered over to town. Though he didn't know much about sailing, he'd been handling powerboats since boyhood. Back when his father had been alive, the Aldens had summered both in New Hampshire and in the Long Island Hamptons. Yachting, water skiing and fishing had always been a way of life.

Rebel had given him the keys to a car the McCades kept parked at the marina. After checking on the *Arabesque,* Josh slid onto the torn seat of the huge, rusting Buick. With a grimace of distaste he wrestled the stubborn transmission into gear and made the harrowing trip to the local grill for lunch.

Afterward he lurched across the highway to the grocery store. Countless people honked their horns or called and waved to him. He could feel himself sinking lower and lower into the seat. Either the McCades were very well known or their dented Buick was a standing joke around town. Probably both.

Later, when he rounded the last buoy on his way back to Gasparilla he found Rebel standing at the end of the dock. While she caught and fastened the line, he tried to figure out if she'd been keeping an eye out for him on purpose. If so, why? Didn't she trust him to handle her boat safely? Or had she *maybe* missed him a little bit?

The last thought was tempting. He watched her keenly as she knelt to rope the cleats. There was no blush on her pretty face, no smile curving that kissable mouth. She looked downright serious.

Which meant she hadn't been waiting for him at all. He was surprised to find how much that realization annoyed him. He'd never thought of himself as the kind of man whose ego needed feminine stroking.

Rebel deftly caught the keys he tossed to her. "How're the repairs going?"

After picking up the grocery bag, he leapt onto the dock beside her. "The electrical system should be ready today. They're starting the fiberglass tomorrow. Three or four days at most.''

''That's great.''

He glanced at her sharply. Was it?

She gestured at the sack. ''Buy something?''

''Shaving cream, razor blades, stuff like that. I didn't plan on staying this long.''

''No, I guess not.'' She fell behind him as he started up the path.

He turned. ''Aren't you coming?''

''I'm waiting for Pop. They should be back any minute.''

''Oh.'' So she *hadn't* been hanging around just because of him.

Not that he cared.

He brooded anyway while walking back to his cottage. Thought about the coolness she'd been exhibiting toward him since he'd gotten back. The way her eyes didn't sparkle anymore when she talked to him. The way he couldn't get her to smile, when it used to be so easy. Had he scared her off with that kiss on the porch?

Come on! Rebel?

Still, he brooded about it while unpacking the groceries. Just as he finished he heard the macaw start screaming. A few minutes later a boat motor roared. Yellow Dog went galloping past his door, heading for the dock.

By the time Josh wandered down himself, the biggest of Pop's charter boats had been made fast at its berth. Pop was stowing equipment in the cabin behind the cockpit while a dark-haired boy rummaged through a cooler in the stern. His pointed pixie face was so like Rebel's that Josh instantly realized that he was her brother, Lee.

Looking up and catching Josh's eye, the boy grinned—Rebel's grin, open and inquisitive. His eyes were the same bright blue. His nose even turned up at the tip, although unlike Rebel's, it was dusted with freckles. Josh guessed that he was twelve or thirteen— a gawky age he himself tended to recall with a shudder. He gestured toward the cooler. "What's in there?"

"Bait." Lee flipped the lid. "Watch this."

The moment he tossed a handful of fish into the water a streak of silver snatched it up and fled. Intrigued, Josh moved closer. "What was that?"

"Tarpon. They wait here to feed."

Lee threw another handful of fish and again the sleek silver body lunged from beneath the dock. Others followed. Yellow Dog stood next to Josh, barking down at the churning water.

Pop clumped over, an unlit cigar between his teeth. "That's enough. Back to work."

Lee obediently reached for the wash bucket.

A burst of laughter brought Josh's attention to the palm-thatched shack at the opposite end of the dock. Rebel was surrounded by a group of men, doing something that was earning her a lot of admiring looks.

Too many.

He strode over to investigate. She smiled when she saw him.

"Josh! Take a look at your supper."

She'd been cleaning fish. Filleting them on a stainless-steel table with a deftly wielded knife. Her audience watched critically, arguing good-naturedly about whose catch was superior.

"No trophies," someone lamented to Josh, who was standing around feeling pretty foolish. "But all of them are really nice, don't you think?"

Josh had no idea.

"Do you still make that blackened tuna with bell-pepper sauce, Rebel?"

Her dimples appeared. "Only for you, Mr. Walsh." She glanced up. "Josh, these are our February regulars."

She supplied their names and Josh shook hands all around. There were four of them of varying ages and backgrounds. One of them, an older man in a white polo shirt, shorts and sandals, didn't release Josh's hand right away.

"Alden? Where from?"

"Rhode Island."

"Yeah, I thought so. You're with Alden-Moore of Providence, right? We've met before. I sit on the board at Hamilton International. We met at their Denver symposium last May."

Memory kicked in. Josh served on so many corporate boards that he couldn't always remember all

the people he met. "Of course. Harper Jennings."
He gave the older man's hand another firm shake.
"Good to see you again."

"You, too." Harper slapped him on the back,
briefly reminding the others what Alden-Moore
stood for.

Josh paid no attention to the interested looks
turned his way. He was used to getting that kind of
reaction whenever the family name was mentioned.
It helped that his father, a tough, visionary real-
estate developer, had managed to parlay a modest
fortune into an empire—Reardon's word—of numerous corporations, foundations and investment
firms before he died.

Harp Jennings, Josh remembered, was a self-
made millionaire, who owned obscene amounts of
Manhattan real estate, a fiber optics company on
the West Coast and controlling interests in numerous Fortune 100 companies. Jennings had enough
money to buy his own resort. What was he doing
here at McCades' Fish Camp, sleeping in a dowdy
little cottage painted salmon pink?

He waited until the others had dispersed to
shower and change for dinner. By then Rebel had
finished filleting the fish and he volunteered to carry
them to the house.

"I'm confused," he told her as they started up
the path.

"About what?"

"Those guys. Harper Jennings, Theodore Walsh. What are they doing here?"

"Fishing, silly."

He switched the bucket to his other hand. The tuna was heavy. "I know, but why here?"

"Well, why not?"

"Because there must be hundreds of other charter boats and fishing guides in the Keys. Why your father? Why this camp in particular? I know Harp Jennings. It surprises me that he would choose to come here, that's all."

Rebel had grown still. An odd little ache had settled around her heart. "You mean, because he's the type who usually stays at some fancy ocean front resort? The kind with brand-new boats? All the amenities we don't have?"

"That's not what I meant."

"Sure it is." Her face was hard.

Josh felt a twinge of exasperated anger. At himself, not her. "Rebel, I'm sorry. I didn't mean for it to sound that way. I was just surprised, that's all."

She didn't answer. Slim shoulders stiff, she led him up the steps and into the house. She gestured toward the sink. "Put the fish there. Then come with me."

They went down the cluttered hall into a room Josh had never seen before. A room brightened by windows and lined with shelves crammed full of books. A huge television flanked by comfortable armchairs stood in one corner. A mahogany desk filled the opposite wall. The telephone system was equipped with a sophisticated answering machine and several outgoing lines. A computer, the latest PC, sat humming nearby.

"We've got a modem, a fax, and we're on the Internet. Use of any equipment is complimentary. So are the cellphones. That way Mr. Jennings can stay in touch with his office whenever he's here."

Josh stared, stunned. He recognized an investment when he saw one.

"Pop had all this put in a few years ago. He updates constantly. Most of our guests are executives taking a few days off for some great blue-water fishing. The best in the world." Her sharp little chin jutted. "Sure, they can afford to stay anywhere they want. But they choose to come here. Pop may not be much to look at, but he's one of the best charterboat captains in the Keys. Especially flats fishing. You don't just buy a boat, get a license and call yourself a flats fisherman. You have to have talent, skill. Pop's got enough of both to take lots of senators and even a few ex-presidents bone fishing every summer. Ask anybody around here. His nearest competitors, the Doughertys, don't get half the bookings he does. I suppose that's the reason people put up with staying in a place like this. Clean, but primitive. Relaxing, but shabby. *Most* people don't seem to care."

"Rebel, wait."

But she was gone.

Groaning, Josh sank into a chair. Putting his head in his hands he massaged his aching temples. He felt as though he'd just been dealt a good, swift clip to the jaw.

Not that he hadn't deserved it, insulting a woman like Rebel. Hurting her. Worst of all was the unpleasant discovery he'd just made about himself, something he would have never believed in a million years: he could come across as an even bigger snob than his cousin Reardon.

Chapter Five

There was no way to apologize. Rebel's father and brother were with her in the kitchen when Josh entered the main house. Rebel was already hard at work cooking. Steam rose from numerous pans. Pots bubbled on the stove. Pop was doing something messy with a cantaloupe over at the counter. The macaw sat on his shoulder, watching with interest. All that was missing to make the pirate image complete was a gold earring and a cutlass, Josh thought.

Lee was dicing red bell peppers on the butcher-block table. For a kid he was pretty good with a knife, Josh noticed. Rebel moved between them, scowling, tasting, giving orders, then crossing back to the stove to stir, season and adjust the burner temperature.

Josh stood in the doorway feeling surprisingly out of place, which was not something he was used to. Damn it, he'd been running his father's business single-handedly for the past eight years! He controlled and invested millions of dollars, and headed a foundation that oversaw numerous charities, scholarships and grants. He dealt with all kinds of people, hundreds of them, every single day of the week. None of them had ever made him feel awkward before.

"Josh, we missed you today." Pop had finally seen him. Reaching for a dish towel, he wiped his hands. Monster squawked and bit his ear. "Coulda used an extra hand in the boat."

"I'm not much on fishing."

"Pshaw! I'll bet you never tried."

"Actually, I have."

"Not in South Florida waters."

Rebel shot her father a warning glance. Pop ignored her. "I'm talkin' about the Gulf Stream. Hell, beyond it. There's nothing like trolling a hundred-year-old shipwreck or hooking a forty-pound grouper. We're after sailfish at the moment. Got a tournament going on with an extra place in the boat since the Beckwiths canceled. Care to come along?"

"Pop—"

"I'll charge half price, and equipment is complimentary."

"Pop—"

"Consider it a beginner's discount."

Josh looked from Pop's twinkling blue eyes into Rebel's disapproving ones. He felt a smile stirring. She was mad, genuinely mad, at the old man. And she was really cute when she was angry. Furthermore, her concern was touching. He'd never had anyone looking out for his wallet before.

"What the heck. I'll give it a shot."

"They're leaving at three o'clock in the morning," Rebel warned.

Josh's smile faded. "You're kidding."

"Do I look like it?"

No, she didn't. "What on earth for?"

"To troll for bait. Be offshore before the sun comes up."

"Rebel packs a hamper and jugs of coffee," Pop added. Oh, McCade was crafty, all right, Josh thought. He knew just how to wheedle.

Josh turned up his palms. "In that case, how can I refuse?"

He felt the waves of Rebel's disapproval battering him throughout dinner. Not that she was angry with him. The looks she kept shooting her father could have cut the man in two.

Pop was obviously used to them, because he paid no mind. He just kept grinning at her and shoveling food into his mouth.

All of them ate boarding-house style at the big table on the porch. Despite Rebel's silent anger the talk was lively. Harp Jennings and his companions were obviously regulars of long standing. They seemed to know everything about the McCade family: that Lee lived with his mother in Michigan during the school year and spent vacations on Gasparilla Key. That Rebel had three stepbrothers who descended on the camp every summer, bringing with them assorted wives and offspring and leaving utter mayhem in their wake.

As for dinner itself, Josh had never tasted anything so good: freshly caught tuna braised to flaky perfection, topped with a roasted red pepper sauce. Parsleyed potatoes and gently steamed asparagus. An outstanding wine as accompaniment.

If anything, Josh decided, folks probably came back to McCades' year after year just for the food. Those oceanfront resorts he'd made out to Rebel as being superior would be hard-pressed to compare.

During dessert, talk turned to strategy behind the next day's fishing. Josh didn't understand much of what was said. There were references to sight trolling, downrigging, monofilaments, loran numbers. He finally managed to catch Rebel's eye.

"You tried to warn me."

"You wouldn't listen."

"Am I going to regret it?"

"You'll have to wait and see." But she was smiling at him, her eyes no longer sparking with anger.

Was he forgiven? He'd always figured she wasn't the type to stay mad for long. Not at Pop, not at him.

The party broke up soon after dessert. A two-thirty wake-up call loomed. Pop muttered something about checking on his charts and disappeared upstairs. Lee cleared the table with a willingness uncommon for a preteen.

Rebel said good-night to the guests and busied herself cleaning the kitchen. Two years ago she'd insisted that Pop buy her an automatic dishwasher. Naturally the cheapskate had refused, but Rebel, fed up with endless pots and pans to scrub, had calmly threatened him with quitting. Moving to the mainland. Leaving him to feed their guests all by himself. Panic-stricken, he'd forked over enough money for a new stove, as well.

She smiled at the memory as she rinsed her hands and hung the dish towel. As if she'd ever contemplate leaving. Gasparilla Key was home. Lord knows she'd tried living in enough other places to realize as much.

"It's a great home," she muttered fondly, surveying the cluttered old kitchen. No matter what Josh said.

Josh. That sad little ache around her heart was back. She'd managed to bury it beneath her anger tonight, the same way she'd been hiding her other feelings from him ever since he'd kissed her on the porch.

Her heart tripped double time at the memory. Oh, man. She wasn't used to being thrown off balance like that. She'd always been able to laugh off everything before. But not where Josh Alden was concerned. He did funny things to her, inside. Things she couldn't control. Things she didn't exactly appreciate. Especially after he'd let her see what kind of a guy he really was. Imagine, suggesting that McCades' was too crummy for the likes of Harp Jennings and his friends!

Her lips thinned. The heck with you, Josh Alden.

Unfortunately, it wasn't that easy to dismiss him from her thoughts. Not at the moment, anyway. Unlike the others, Josh hadn't retired to his rooms after dinner. Instead he'd shut himself up in the study to use the telephone. Heaven help her, but just knowing he was in the house made her feel all restless and jumpy. Unable to sit still. Like Yellow Dog scratching at fleas.

The thought made her burst out laughing. Instantly the ache around her heart lifted.

The heck with Josh Alden, she decided again, much more forcibly this time. The heck with everything. It was Friday night and she was going to go dancing. She would return home in time to brew coffee for the fishing crew at two o'clock, then head off to bed. Let Pop do what he wanted with Josh Alden's wallet. What did she care?

"Rebel?"

Damn! Just the sound of his voice managed to

send a shiver rippling over her skin, no matter what she'd just decided. She whirled, but not before pasting on an uncaring smile. "Hmm?"

"My uncle may call tomorrow while I'm gone. His name's Archer Tate. Will you let him know how the sailboat's doing?"

"Sure. Matter of fact, I'll do better than that. I'm probably going to see Bo Duffy tonight. I'll ask him how far he got today."

"Bo Duffy? The boat mechanic?"

"Yep." She plopped onto a stool and began pulling on her sneakers. "He's always at Callahan's on Friday night."

"Callahan's? What's that?"

"A tiki bar. Over at the Long Key marina."

"You're going there now?"

She nodded and felt him nail her with his eyes. Did he practice that intensely brooding look in front of a mirror, she wondered, or did it just come naturally to all darkly handsome men?

"What do folks do at a tiki bar?"

"Drink. Play darts. I know the guys in the band, so I thought I'd do some dancing." She said it breezily, as if she often went alone and wasn't self-conscious about appearing without a date—probably because she never had to worry about a lack for eager partners.

Josh could well imagine that she didn't have a problem in that respect. An image of her flirting, laughing and dancing with a lot of different men snaked unpleasantly through his mind. Damn it, he wasn't jealous. Just in a foul mood. He'd made a courtesy call to his uncle just now only to end up talking with Tracy instead. She'd wanted to know all about the McCades' camp, demanding a detailed description of the rest of Rebel's family. Her supercilious tone had reminded Josh all too uncomfortably of the disparaging thing she'd said to Rebel earlier.

No wonder he was feeling grumpy.

Finished with her sneakers, Rebel bounced off the stool and slipped into the worn denim jacket hanging on a hook by the door. Peering at her reflection in the glass oven door, she combed her fingers through her short, dark hair. Tousled, pretty, humming beneath her breath, she dug through a drawer and came up with a pair of gold hoop earrings. A bold red line from a lipstick hunted up in similar fashion followed.

Josh watched, fascinated. He'd never seen a woman ready herself for an evening out from the contents of a kitchen drawer. Only Rebel could pull it off. Only Rebel could look so sexy with her dark hair casually fluffed and heavy gold hoops dancing in her ears. She was wearing tight-fitting white silk pants that ended several inches above her sunbrowned ankles. A scoop-necked tank top of pale cream revealed her slim collarbones and the curve of her breasts.

She looked like a teenager in the denim jacket

and sneakers, but there was no way Josh could think of her like that. No, she was all woman, slim and feisty and infinitely desirable.

"Well?" She propped her hands on her hips and cocked an eyebrow at him.

Breathtaking. Seductive. A woman made for sweeping off to bed. He itched to peel her out of those clothes, to feel the silky coolness of her skin beneath his hands. "You look, ah, very nice."

"Not that. Are you coming or not?"

He stared. "To Callahan's? Am I invited?"

"Yeah, I guess."

"Why? Feeling sorry for me?"

She snorted. "Hardly. Listen up, Alden. This is not a date."

"I didn't think it was."

"Good. As long as we got that straight." She scribbled a note to her father, then glanced at Josh over the tip of her pen. "Man. I forgot about tomorrow. Pop's planning to leave around three. You need sleep—"

Josh caught her by the hip and propelled her toward the door. "I'm a big boy. Let's go."

Despite its name, Callahan's didn't resemble any Irish pub of Josh's acquaintance. This one was no more than a plywood shack built over the water, with palm fronds rustling overhead. Neon flamingo signs blinked at the door. Blenders whirred as countless frozen daiquiris were whipped up for the tourists. There were locals as well, crowding the booths and the dance floor. Josh could tell who the locals were because they all seemed to know Rebel.

"Hiya, sweetie!"

"Man, you look good enough to eat."

"Hey, what's this? Since when do you bring a date?"

Disappointed looks followed her inside. Rebel ignored them all. A band with a Latino beat was churning out dance numbers on a small stage in one corner. The atmosphere was electric, fun. The floor was packed, but Rebel, grabbing Josh's hand, pulled him through the noisy throng.

They found a table on the outside terrace. The breeze was cool, salty. The music throbbed, a relentlessly tropical beat. Rebel tapped her foot as she slid into her chair.

A young waitress crossed over to them, eyeing Josh with unabashed interest. "Hey, Reb. What'll ya have?"

"Lime daiquiri." She looked in inquiry at Josh.

"Vodka. On the rocks."

Rebel propped her elbows on the table when they were alone and regarded him very earnestly. "So, what do you think?"

"Not bad," he answered truthfully. "Very colorful."

"What do you do in Providence when you go out?"

He grinned. "This time of year? Try to keep warm."

"You're not much on bars," she guessed.

"No, not really."

"So how do you show your date a good time?"

"Dinner, usually. Maybe a show, if we're in New York. Drinks in some quiet place as a prelude to bed."

He'd said that just to see her reaction. He wanted to know if he could make those beautiful eyes widen and that kissable mouth of hers fall open.

He should have known better. Rebel merely settled more comfortably into her chair. Tossing her dark, cropped hair, she fired off a wicked grin. "Yeah? So how much does that set you back?"

It was an effort to keep his lips from twitching. She really was unflappable. "Couple of hundred dollars. Maybe more."

"Man." She shook her head. "Things sure are cheaper in the Keys."

Now what did she mean by that? Was she tossing him a hint? Or just making a casual observation?

Before he could ask, Rebel bounced out of her chair. "Come on, Providence. Let's dance."

Hauling him along behind her, she waded onto the crowded floor. The band had abandoned its driving calypso beat for a bluesy number led by a tenor sax. Bad choice, Josh thought. Rebel had already warned him that they were not on a date. She'd never agree to such a slow, intimate dance.

Wrong again.

Rising up on her toes, Rebel wrapped her arms around his neck. All of his preconceived notions instantly fled from his mind. Honestly, the woman didn't have a shy bone in her body.

And what an enormously sexy body it was, Josh was reminded as he slipped his hands around her waist. Looking down into her eyes, watching her reaction, he brought her closer until her slim, curvy body fitted tightly to his.

"Mmm," she murmured in his ear. "Maybe it wasn't so dumb inviting you, after all."

"Wait a minute. I thought you said you didn't feel sorry for me."

She unlinked her arms long enough to lay a finger against his lips. "Shh. Don't talk." And then she did what she'd been itching to do for a long time. She brushed her fingers ever so lightly across his gorgeous, manly jaw.

Maybe she hadn't intended as much, but it was a very seductive caress. Immediately the look in Josh's eyes changed. No longer lazy, they were now watching her in a way that was focused, intent.

Something shivered through Rebel's blood in response. Earlier, they'd joked about how he went about taking women to bed. His casual remarks were suddenly very much on her mind. The thought of bed, and the feel of his strong, muscular body against hers, left her imagining some extremely disturbing things about Josh Alden of Providence,

Rhode Island. Things that made the color rise high in her cheeks until she found herself blushing scarlet, right in front of him.

"Oh, no," she squeaked, aware that she'd probably given herself away.

"What?" He was being a gentleman, but of course he knew.

Rebel hadn't realized she'd voiced her dismay out loud. But for heaven's sake, she wasn't used to finding herself tongue-tied around a man, or fantasizing about going to bed with him while standing in the middle of a crowded dance floor! She didn't like it, and she wished like heck Josh would quit making her feel this way.

Using all her willpower, she managed to keep from bolting, thus humiliating herself completely. But the moment the dance ended she scurried back to their table. Josh followed, lips twitching, and watched with raised brows as she downed the rest of her drink in a single swallow. Plopping into her seat, she wiggled around like a child who simply couldn't sit still.

Josh bit his lip in a continued effort to keep from grinning. So, he'd finally found a way to pitch a curve at Rebel McCade. Slow dancing, keeping their bodies center to center, gave her about as much as a snowball's chance of pretending she didn't feel the pull of attraction between them.

Not that he intended to take advantage of his discovery. The way Rebel looked in those clinging silk pants, the way she'd felt in his arms while they danced, warned him he'd be playing with fire. No way was he going to get burned.

Instead he leaned back and hooked an arm casually over his chair, behaving as though he'd been totally oblivious to any sparks arcing between them. "We haven't talked much, but your brother Lee, seems like a pretty nice kid."

She regarded him blankly.

"Your brother? Lee McCade? He lives in Michigan during the school year, doesn't he?"

Rebel's expression cleared. "Yeah. With my mother."

"I take it your parents are divorced."

"Ages ago. My mom's from Ann Arbor originally." She was very grateful for something to talk about to curb her dangerous thoughts.

"How did she end up down here?"

"She went to college in Atlanta."

"Why Atlanta? Because she'd read *Gone with the Wind?*"

Rebel smiled, pleased that he'd remembered. "Yup. You know what? She absolutely hated it."

"Really?"

"Ironic, isn't it?"

"Why?"

"Who knows? Maybe because it wasn't warm enough after all those winters in Ann Arbor. Anyway, she tried Miami next. Came down to the Keys one weekend, and that's when she met Pop. Believe it or not, he was really good-looking back then. I've seen pictures.''

Josh didn't doubt it. Pop's daughter was a beauty. ''So they got married, and after a while you came along?''

''Right.''

The waitress brought drinks and Josh waited until she was gone. ''So what about your brother? How old is he?''

''He'll be thirteen in June.''

''That's a big gap.''

''I know. Fourteen years. I think my parents' marriage started falling apart when I was ten. That's when my mom first took me to Michigan for the summer. She couldn't stand the humidity, the mosquitoes, the boredom of summers here in the Keys. I think by then she'd grown disenchanted with the whole idea of the South. You know how it is. Nothing's ever the way it seems in books.''

''Did you like Ann Arbor?''

''I guess. But I couldn't wait to get home. I practically counted the minutes until Labor Day. Pop didn't like it, either, being alone so much. I suppose that's why something had to give. Lee was their last attempt at reconciliation. Mom named him after Robert E. Lee. Despite everything, she was still loyal to the South. Or her romantic ideals, anyway.''

''But not enough to stay.''

Rebel shrugged her slim shoulders.

"So Lee ended up in Michigan with your mother and you chose to stay here with your father."

"Kids always have to make choices when their parents split. You can't keep them both, especially when they live so far apart. Don't get me wrong." Rebel stirred the straw in the remains of her drink. "I get along fine with my mom and stepfamily. So does Lee. But I chose Pop and the Keys, and I've never regretted it. My mom's the one who lost out." Her eyes weren't hard or resentful. They were soft, very loving.

Josh sipped his drink, enjoying their honest conversation, enjoying her. "I take it you've never been married yourself."

Rebel laughed, shaking her head.

"Why not? Are you waiting for a man just like your father to come along?"

She hooted. "Yeah, right." Then she gave his question some thought. "Actually, the guys around here are *too much* like Pop. I wouldn't take any of them on a bet."

Josh leaned forward. "So who would you take?"

"I'm not really sure." She stuck out her lower lip, considering. "I guess the man I marry would have to be—" She broke off abruptly because she'd been about to say "—a lot like you."

Right. Josh Alden, with his wealth and social snobbery, was definitely *not* a suitable candidate for matrimony. While Rebel didn't exactly object to his money, she couldn't honestly say that she yearned for the life of leisure an Alden wife would probably be expected to lead. Winters in the Bahamas, summers in some ivy-league town, attending those Broadway plays Josh had mentioned and dining at the exclusive clubs he no doubt belonged to.

And don't forget Tates for in-laws.

Eeeewww, as Tracy would say.

Resting her chin on her hand, Rebel took a long, assessing look at Josh. What was it that she found so attractive about him? Disregarding, of course, his fantastic good looks?

For one thing, she liked the way he seemed so comfortable with himself. He was a calm man, dependable and strong. Just being around him was pleasant.

What else?

Well, she couldn't deny that she was attracted to him in a very physical way. That he made her insides hum like no man ever had.

But it was more than that. A lot more. Josh had a way of making a woman feel…special. Appreciated. As though—

"What's the matter?

She lifted her gaze to his. "Huh?"

"You're staring. Do I have corn chips between my teeth?"

She shook her head to clear it. She wanted to kick herself. She was acting…moony. She'd never mooned over a man before and she wasn't going to start now. Certainly not over a blue-blooded Alden of Providence, Rhode Island.

She regarded him contritely. "I'm sorry. What were we talking about?"

"You were going to tell me what sort of man you'd like to marry."

She blurted the first thing that came to mind. "I don't care, as long as he likes to fish." Ugh. That was pretty lame, Reb.

Josh rattled the ice in his drink. "Well, that rules me out, doesn't it?"

"Thank goodness," she said, laughing heartily. No problem, she thought. I'm in control. Piece of cake. "Come on, Providence." She hauled him out of his chair. "Let's see how long you can last on the dance floor this time."

Actually, he managed pretty well. She should have remembered that he was in outstanding physical condition. In fact, she was the one who ended up collapsing in her chair, out of breath, at the end of the set.

"Phew! I think I've had it."

"You should have told me you wanted to quit."

She looked at him, her mouth partly open, still breathing heavily. "Ha. As if you'd let me."

He deliberately kept his gaze from the tempting rise and fall of her breasts. "You could have forced me. Tried that headlock you pulled this morning."

"Oh, yeah, I forgot. You were a real wimp about that," she gloated.

He tugged her hair, leaning in close. "I'd like a rematch sometime."

Oh, how her blood started singing just from the look in his eyes! What are you doing to me, Josh Alden?

She waited until he'd seated himself across from her, where his nearness couldn't rattle her so easily, then gave him a smirk and a toss of her head. "How about now?" She propped her arm on the table. "Care to wrestle, Providence?"

He laughed mockingly. "No way on earth. You haven't got a chance."

"You're just chicken."

Leaning forward, he cupped his hand around her wrist, his fingers sliding in a whispery caress over her rose-petal skin. Beneath his thumb he could feel the wild throb of her pulse. His eyes lifted to hers. "Believe me, I'm not chicken."

Far from it. At the moment he wanted very much to feel more of that silky skin, every heated inch of it, in fact. Not cowardice, but caution, was keeping him back.

But he couldn't quite bring himself to break the contact between them. Rebel's eyes were wide, a dark, seductive blue that twisted his gut into knots and brought a fiery surge of desire raging through his blood. He wanted her, damn it. And he was pretty damned sure that she wanted him.

So what was holding them back? Why not take

her home, tear those skimpy clothes from her lovely body and bury himself deep inside her?

The thought had him groaning. Tightening his fingers around her wrist he tugged her to her feet. He'd have to settle for another dance, quickly, before his control snapped. "Come on. Last one."

Rebel followed him wordlessly onto the floor. She felt the heat of him burn her like licking flames wherever they touched. Want and need poured through her like a savage storm tide. It had been stupid of her to challenge him to something physical, even if it was only arm wrestling. Every time he touched her he made her go all wild and weak inside.

He was right. She wouldn't have had a chance.

Chapter Six

Rebel was surprised to find Harp Jennings in the kitchen the next morning. Startled, she glanced at the clock. "Nine-thirty? But I thought— Wasn't the boat supposed to leave at three?"

"It was and it did." Harper sounded gloomy. "But I wasn't on it."

Rebel's expression softened with understanding. "Ulcers acting up again?"

He sighed and nodded.

"Let me fix you something to eat." She knew from past experience what would help. "And for goodness' sake, put away that coffee! You know it only makes things worse!"

"Now, Rebel, I'm fond of you, but that doesn't give you the right—"

"To sound like your wife. I know, you've told me that before. Often." Grinning, she plucked the mug from his grasp and poured the contents down the drain. "But she definitely knows what's good for you, and I know it, too, and you'll just have to accept that, especially if you want to be out on the water tomorrow. Only two days left in the tournament, remember."

"Okay, okay, you win."

He watched, scowling, as she went about fixing his breakfast. "Got in late last night, didn't you? You and Alden."

"We went to Callahan's."

"After one o'clock before you came home, wasn't it?"

Rebel had always been fond of Harper, enjoyed talking with him, but she didn't want the conversation veering toward Josh. She didn't want Harp or anyone else thinking they'd been out on a date or anything like that.

She shrugged. "It was dark. You can't race a boat home in the dark."

"No, I guess not. Um, Reb...don't you think those eggs've been stirred enough?"

Looking down, she realized she'd whipped them into a foamy froth. Quickly she poured them into the pan and watched while they sizzled. Armed with a spatula, she thought about that long, slow boat ride home. The night had been clear with a soft, tropical breeze. The sky had been awash with stars that were reflected in the quiet bay like diamond dust. Josh had stood at the bow of the boat helping to navigate through the darkness, and Rebel had watched him from the console with her heart aching fit to burst.

Only his shadow had been visible in the dim starlight, but she'd looked her fill without fear of discovery, greedily memorizing every inch of those wide shoulders, that dark, curly hair, the way he stood with his hands in his pockets, so watchful and still.

Lord knows Rebel had never been one to keep still for long, but Josh certainly could. Lately she'd come to realize how much she liked the way his stillness could wash over her whenever he was near, creeping slowly into her heart, her soul, filling her up. Making her feel calm and easy, too, in a way she so rarely was.

But just as easily, with only a certain look or smile, he could destroy her peace of mind completely, making her feel like Yellow Dog walking around with his hackles raised, restless, ill at ease, sensing something unusual in the air, only not knowing exactly what.

Like walking on eggs, Rebel thought, giving those in the pan a savage flip. Exasperating. Infuriating. She wasn't used to feeling like this. And she sure as heck didn't care for it, either.

"Wonder how they're doing," Harp mused.

Rebel set a plate in front of him. "Bet you're

hoping they aren't having any luck. That they won't win the tournament without you.''

"I'm a real SOB, aren't I?"

They exchanged fond smiles.

"What would you do if Josh Alden brought home the trophy catch?" Rebel asked wickedly. Seeing him reach for the saltshaker she slapped his hand away. "Bland, remember?"

"Even the eggs?"

"Especially the eggs."

"Aww, hell. Okay. But only because I intend to make the trip tomorrow. As for Alden, he isn't going to bring home any winning sailfish. Not after he's been up all night at Callahan's." He twinkled at her. "You didn't happen to do that on purpose, did you?"

"Yeah, right."

Harp's amusement faded. "They're not going to win without me. Are they?"

"Of course not."

"What about beginner's luck? It's possible, you know."

Rebel shook her head. "Not when it comes to a tournament. Pop's little black book is going to win that for you, not Josh Alden."

Harp brightened visibly. "You're right. That black book of his is what brings me back year after year, hon. Oh, and cooking like this." He homed in on the saltshaker again but a warning glance from Rebel made him think twice. "And you're right in saying nobody has that kind of beginner's luck, not even a guy like Alden.''

''Oh?'' Rebel propped her hip against the counter and folded her arms very casually in front of her. ''Leads a charmed life, does he?''

''I'll say.'' Harp spoke around a mouthful of eggs. ''Took over the family business when his father died eight or nine years ago. Everything was already in perfect working order, so young Josh barely had to get his feet wet.''

''What exactly does he do? This Alden-Moore company you mentioned—''

''It's a charitable foundation set up by Josh's grandfather, Stanford Moore. It started small, but it's worth millions today. They underwrite scholarships, concerts, not-for-profit productions. They support the arts, endow university chairs, you name it. Their profits come from other companies—telecommunications, primarily— but they've diversified over the past decade. Don't let Josh's slow fuse fool you. He's as hard hitting as they come.''

''I had no idea.''

''Why should you?''

Yes, why should she? Living down here in the remote Florida Keys, worlds away from Josh Alden's multimillion-dollar empire, how could she know how much he was really worth? And she'd had the nerve to flirt with him, dream about him, drag him to a rundown little tiki bar for daiquiris and dancing!

Rebel, you're a hoot.

The fishing boat returned while Rebel was in town running errands. She hated the way her heart gave a crazy leap when she steered her skiff around the mangrove trees and saw Pop's big sportfisher tied up at the dock. Ted Walsh and his partners were hauling out their catch for Harp Jennings to admire. Lee was washing down equipment while Pop tinkered around in the cockpit. There was no sign of Josh.

"Gone to bed," Pop told her when she asked. "You had no business keepin' him up all night."

Rebel ignored the comment. Pop was in a bad mood. According to Lee, the Dougherty boys been boasting on the shortwave about the size of the sail-fish one of their clients had hauled in. So far, it was the biggest on record. No one on Pop's boat had hooked anything close.

"Mr. Walsh got a monster wahoo, but that's all." Lee rinsed out the bait bucket and inverted it over a piling. "Pop said Mr. Jennings might've gotten somethin' if he'd been there. You know he's always lucky when he's trollin'."

"He'll be back tomorrow. How about Josh? Mr. Alden? How'd he do?"

"No sailfish. But he did hook a cobia."

"Yeah? Did he bring it in?" Cobia, Rebel knew, put up a pretty good fight.

"Yeah, finally." Lee grinned. "Pop says he's gonna be sore tomorrow."

"I'll bet." Rebel could see a corner of Josh's cottage through the trees. She couldn't blame him for going to bed so early after a long day's fishing and being up all hours the night before.

She wasn't disappointed, she told herself. She didn't miss him at all.

Maybe he'd show up for supper....

He didn't. Cottage number four remained dark for the rest of the day. Pop figured Josh would probably sleep straight through until morning.

"I'll get him up when it's time to leave," he told Rebel after dinner. "We're castin' off at three."

"You'll do no such thing."

"Now, Reb—"

"No, Pop. He didn't specifically tell you he wanted to go out again, did he?"

"Well, no, but—"

"Then you're going to let him sleep. And that means you're not going to charge him for another day's fishing, either."

"But, Rebel! I got me an empty berth, and tomorrow's the last day! If I don't win that tournament, them Dougherty boys will!"

"It's happened before."

"You're heartless, you know that?" He stumped after her as she hung the dish towel and left the kitchen. "I just gotta win this one, honey. I need that prize money bad and you know it."

Rebel sighed. Whenever Pop sounded this woebegone she could almost feel sorry for him. Actually, he did have a point. The prize money that the winning charter-boat captain stood to gain would be enough for the down payment on the new boat Pop had been wanting for more than a year. With greater horsepower he'd be able to cut his traveling time to the Gulf Stream and beyond by two or three hours, opening up a whole new range of fishing opportunities for his clients. A good business decision, but one that simply wasn't possible without a win.

"I know five in the boat's pushin' it, but we need all the help we can get at this point."

He sounded so genuinely unhappy that Rebel actually did feel sorry for him. But he was going to have to succeed without Josh. She told him so, again.

"Okay, okay. But remember, it ain't just the boat we'll be givin' up. It's a new roof for the house."

"Big deal. We fixed the worst of the leaks, didn't we?"

"What about a new outboard for your skiff?"

"I can live with the one I've got."

"And stuff for Lee. I owe his mother a bundle."

"Pop, you haven't had to pay child support since Mom remarried. Do us both a favor. If you need money so bad, play the lottery."

He glared at her. She liked to rib him about the lottery because she knew he was too cheap to fork out a few dollars for tickets. "Okay. Maybe I will."

"Wow, you really are feeling low, aren't you?"

He didn't answer. She took pity on him and gave him a daughterly pat on the back. "Look, I'll speak to Josh as soon as I see him. He might even show up for something to eat later on. Maybe he'll go out with you day after tomorrow if the *Arabesque* isn't ready."

"Bah. The tournament'll be over by then."

"There'll be another one starting. And one after that. All winter long."

"Not sailfish." Sailfish were Pop's specialty. So were marlin and bone fish.

"The ladies' billfish tournament starts next week," Rebel reminded him.

Pop snorted. She knew he disliked taking women out fishing. But that was only because he hated it when they showed him up.

"I'll talk to Josh," Rebel repeated over her shoulder and left the room.

But he never showed up for supper, or even for breakfast the following morning. Rebel waded through her chores, cleaned Monster's cage and gave Yellow Dog a bath. She kept an eye out for Josh while straightening up the other cottages, but the shutters in number four remained closed.

Finished with housekeeping, she passed his door on the way back to the house. As she did, she thought she heard a groan coming from inside. Setting down her mop and bucket, she knocked quietly.

"Josh?"

Sure enough, he was groaning. Yellow Dog whined. Rebel knocked again, harder.

"Josh? You okay?"

The door creaked open. Josh stood in boxer shorts and a T-shirt, glowering at her. Rebel burst out laughing the moment she saw him.

"Stop it, Rebel. It isn't funny."

"Yes, it is. You look like the worst kind of tourist."

"Go away. I'm not in the mood for insults."

Instead she followed him inside, still laughing.

"Rebel, please—"

She put a hand over her mouth to stop her giggles. He really did look bad. His chestnut curls were stuck together from the saltwater. His skin was sunburnt to a crisp. He walked around with his aching arms held straight out in front of him in the classic beginning fisherman's stance of "reel cramps."

"Heard you did battle with a cobia." Rebel still had her hand over her mouth. "Kinda sore, huh?"

"I feel like death warmed over." Groaning, he sank into a chair. He looked battle shocked, drained, completely worn out.

Rebel's amusement gave way to a sudden urge to run her fingers through his disheveled curls and press her lips to his sunburned brow. She knew she shouldn't, but she couldn't resist touching him. Just once. Just a little.

"Oh, man." His head fell forward as she stepped behind him to massage his aching shoulders. "That feels great."

"No wonder. You're tied up in knots."

"Tell me about it."

She wished she could tell him a lot of things. Like how much her heart was singing because she was doing something useful for him. And what it did to her, inside, to touch him like this, to feel the tension in his shoulders easing beneath the pressure of her hands. Those wide, fascinating shoulders. She loved the way they strained against his T-shirt. The way his hair curled boyishly at the nape of his neck. The way he looked to her right now despite his misery: big, muscular, totally masculine.

Desire stirred strongly within her. Thrown off balance by the force of it, she stepped away.

"Rebel?"

"Hmm?" Darn it, her voice was all wobbly, just like her knees.

"Don't ever let your dad talk me into going fishing again."

"I won't. I promise." She bit her lip, hiding her hurt. He hadn't felt a thing. Nothing. She had to remember what he thought of her, of her background, her social standing. Even if he were on the lookout for companionship, she definitely wasn't in the running.

Taking a deep breath she willed herself to smile. "Know what you need?"

"What?"

"A shower. Breakfast. A totally relaxing day."

"All in that order?"

"All in that order."

"Okay." He rose slowly to his feet. "I'll do the first, you take care of the second. Then let's see what happens with the third."

Was he actually suggesting that they spend time together? The prospect made her smile break out for real. "Deal. Come on up to the house when you're ready."

Josh didn't move until the cottage door closed behind her. After the way she'd touched him just now he'd definitely need a shower, an icy cold one.

Rebel was checking the oil in her skiff when Josh came down to the dock. He looked worlds better after a shower and breakfast and several mugs of coffee. His sunburn had faded from beacon red to pinkish tan and his newly washed hair glinted gold where it brushed the collar of his polo shirt. Top-Siders, sunglasses and khaki shorts completed a very pleasing, outdoorsy image.

Rebel bent over the engine, messing with the dipstick just to keep her hands busy and her attention off him. "Nice to see you human again."

"Thanks. I think. Breakfast was great. I feel a hundred percent better."

"Good. Do you suppose you can handle some more sun today?"

"Depends on what you have in mind."

She kept on fussing with the outboard. Watching her, he tried not to smile. Didn't she know that she didn't have to hesitate when asking him to spend time with her? He wasn't about to tell her no. In that skimpy tank top and cutoffs, with her pixie face framed by wide sunglasses, she looked so appealing that he'd gladly accompany her anywhere.

"I thought you might enjoy a tour of the back-country."

"The what?"

She gestured toward the water. "Out there. It's what we call the bay."

He couldn't resist teasing her. "Hmm. I'm not sure if I'm up to it."

Her head came up. Behind the sunglasses her eyes went carefully blank. "That's okay. I understand."

"Now wait a minute. Who said I refused? Got any sunblock?"

She dug around in her pack. "A little."

"How about food?"

She nudged the cooler with the toe of her sneaker.

"Bug spray?"

"A brand-new can."

"Ship-to-shore radio?"

She realized at that point that he was teasing her.

A relieved smile peeked out. "I suppose you don't want to get stranded again, huh?"

Actually, the thought was appealing. This time he wouldn't have to share her with Reardon.

"There's no way we'll get stranded, Josh. Once the tide goes out we can pretty much wade home."

"Oh." Too bad.

Ten minutes later they were speeding across the water with Gasparilla Key behind them and the shallow channels and mangrove swamps of the Florida Bay ahead.

"Are we headed anyplace in particular?"

Rebel shrugged. "Could be."

"A secret, is it?"

"Let's just say it's for locals only. Tourists and weekenders have no idea how to get there."

Josh settled back, liking the idea of letting Rebel take him wherever she pleased. He couldn't remember the last time he'd spent an entire day not knowing exactly where he was going, what he would be doing, who he'd be seeing and why. Unheard of, really, to sit back and enjoy the sparkling bright sunshine with no timetables to keep, save those of the outgoing tide. No telephones out here, no meetings to attend or endless problems to solve.

It was a strange sensation. One he definitely liked.

"There's only one problem."

Rebel frowned. "What?"

"Isn't your father going to mind that you're taking the whole day off to show me around?"

"Nah. I'm on vacation. Lee's taking my place as deckhand this week."

"For somebody on vacation you still manage to put in a load of working hours."

"What do you mean?"

He raised a hand to count on his fingers. "Getting up at two in the morning to see the boat off. Keeping the guest houses clean and fixing breakfast and dinner for a minimum of six every day. I've also seen you tinkering with the boats or repairing something in the house or out on the grounds for hours on end."

She laughed with genuine amusement. "You call that work?"

"Isn't it?"

"Josh, nothing's work if you enjoy it."

"Is that so?"

"Sure. Haven't you figured that out yet?"

"No." His tone had gone noticeably flat. Rebel looked at him, surprised. Maybe being a millionaire wasn't all that easy, she mused. Maybe Josh had to work way too hard at being one. She hadn't known him very long, but she'd already noticed how he'd started to mellow, slowly but surely, since coming to Gasparilla Key.

Since he obviously could use a few more weeks of rest and relaxation, she tossed him an improbable challenge. "Tell you what. You stay here for the rest of the winter, do my work for me, and I'll take over your responsibilities in Providence. In a month or so we'll get together and compare notes. Find out which one of us worked the hardest."

"No contest. You'd win hands down. This is paradise compared to my office."

She grinned. "Yeah? Want to put your money where your mouth is?"

"Please, don't tempt me."

"I thought you hated fishing."

"Fish, Ms. McCade, are nothing compared to managing scores of temperamental underlings." Actually, sending Rebel to Providence wasn't such a madcap idea. Josh had to grin, imagining the stir she'd cause bouncing into Alden-Moore with her boundless good cheer. He could name at least a dozen people on his staff who would benefit enormously from just half her energy.

He realized suddenly what he liked the most about Rebel. The fact that she was never still. She was always popping out of her chair to tackle something difficult, talking a mile a minute with her hands and laughing more often than not. She was a whirlwind, impossible to pin down.

He sighed dramatically, his eyes twinkling. "Sorry. It would never work. My liability insurance doesn't cover hurricanes in the workplace."

"You clown." She reached over the side to splash him. Before he could retaliate she cut the engine and turned the skiff into a narrow waterway between banks of waving seagrass.

"Okay, we're here. Time to be quiet."

Josh was instantly intrigued. They seemed to have left the real world behind and entered a primordial jungle. The channel twisted and turned. Aging mangroves formed a canopy over their heads. There was no sound save the slap and gurgle of the tide against the hull.

"Here." Rebel handed him a pair of binoculars. "If you're interested in birds, this is the place to look."

Reaching under the seat she pulled out a long pole and pushed off against the current. Without speaking she pointed out egrets, great blue herons, an osprey that slammed into the water a short distance ahead and took off with a good-size trout in his talons.

"Rebel, this is great."

"I knew you'd be impressed."

"Believe me, I am."

They spoke in whispers.

"Josh, over there!"

She sounded so excited that he whipped the binoculars around and was rewarded by the extremely rare sight of a roseate spoonbill wading among the mangrove roots.

"Man, this is incredible."

Rebel's heart swelled. No way could she feel inadequate around Josh as long as the two of them were out here. Not when they were surrounded by so much natural beauty. And it warmed her through and through to know he could appreciate it as much as she did.

They turned a corner. The vegetation pressed close. Josh leaned toward her. "Think we'll see any alligators?"

"You never know. Maybe. Did you know we have crocodiles, too?"

"Go on."

"No, really. Unfortunately they're nearly extinct."

"Ever seen one yourself?"

Her face fell. "No. I've heard them calling, though. Once, when Lee and I were camping out a few summers ago. We heard them on the far side of the island. They have five or six different calls. They don't sound the least bit like alligators."

"Were you able to get close to them?"

"Nope. There were poachers around, so we thought better of leaving camp. Luckily they never knew we were there."

"Real poachers? The kind that carry guns?"

"Um-hmm."

He thought about asking her if she'd been scared, but already knew what she would say. Nothing seemed to unsettle this woman—unless it was slow dancing with him.

Rebel was busy again with the push pole and missed his smile. Looking ahead, Josh saw that the narrow channel had opened into a broad cove. The glass-clear water deepened. A strong current tugged at the turtle grass below.

Leaning hard into the pole, Rebel beached the skiff on the sandy side of a small island. Hand on her hip, she grinned at him. "Welcome, Mr. Alden, to one of the few places in the backcountry with its own private beach."

"Another perk for hanging with the locals, hmm? Here, I'll carry the cooler."

"You can leave it for now. Unless you're hungry already?"

"Starved."

"Good. I packed a big lunch."

They unloaded the skiff, kicked off their shoes and spread their towels in the sand. With his wrists propped on his updrawn knees, Josh looked around with interest. "Where does that path go?"

"The one between the trees? I'd planned to take you there after lunch. It leads through a really pristine stretch of hammock."

"Of what?"

"Our original forest. Hardwood trees and a canopy, a few wild orchids. It's the way Florida looked when Ponce de Leon arrived."

"Sounds great, but only if you brought along the bug spray."

"Believe me, I never go anywhere without it."

"I noticed you brought masks and flippers."

"Just in case you wanted to do some snorkeling."

He studied the slow-moving water. "Anything to see down there?"

"Sure, when the tide comes in. Of course it's better out on the reef, but we might be able to scare up something interesting."

"The water's so clear."

Rebel sighed. "Not as clear as it used to be. When Pop was a boy you could see thirty feet and more straight down. He said being out on a boat was like gliding over glass, or flying. You could look way, way down into submarine canyons and see every color of the rainbow. It must have been something. Now everything's murky green."

"So what happened?"

"The Everglades are dying." Rebel shrugged, but her voice was anything but casual. "So is the bay."

He shifted to look at her. "How do you mean?"

"Agricultural runoff, human encroachment, chemical spills, stuff like that makes the turtle grass die off. Once it does you get algae bloom, which clouds the water and sends the marine life scurrying. Or kills it outright. It used to be so different, back when I was a kid."

Josh could hear the throbbing regret in her voice and was touched by the fact that she cared so much. Rebel never seemed to do anything, feel anything, tackle anything, in halves. She gave passionately, felt wholeheartedly, about every facet of her life.

She was sitting beside him with her legs drawn up, her pointed chin resting on top of her knees. Her gaze was turned toward the water, but when Josh wrapped his fingers around her upper arm she whirled to face him. He saw that her blue eyes were huge with hurt. They sliced through him, to the heart.

"You know, I don't think I've ever seen you sad before."

"Really?"

"No." And he didn't like it.

Her lips curved. "Come on, Josh. Everybody gets a little down now and then."

"Not you." His voice was rough because he felt so strongly about it. "You should always be happy. Laughing. Anyone who makes Rebel McCade sad should be charged with a federal crime."

That had her smiling again, just as he'd hoped. Not only for her sake, but for his. Smiling back at her, he tightened his hold on her arm and tipped her slowly toward him. Without even knowing that he planned to, he covered her laughing mouth with his own.

The kiss was a jolt, a needy thing that sizzled like lightning between them. Rebel felt the heat of it, of that bold, caressing mouth, slamming through her clear to her toes. She gasped, then sighed, a breathy sound in the back of her throat as shock gave way to delight. Pleasure seeped through her veins, along her nerve ends, into her very bones. Only Josh could make her feel so much, with nothing more than the touch of his mouth.

His head dipped as he deepened the kiss. His hand moved across her bare shoulder to curl around her nape. His other hand dropped to her hip, splaying there so that he could draw her body fully against him.

That was when Rebel knew what it meant to be drowning.

So did Josh. He was steeped in sensation, in her, in the satin softness of her skin and the sunshine scent that was Rebel's alone. Her warmth poured through him, giving way to heat so that within moments he found himself teetering on that fine, painful line between want and need, pleasure and desire.

He knew he should end the kiss before he lost control. He heard the sexy sounds she was making deep in her throat and felt the wild beat of her pulse beneath his thumb, which rested ever so lightly against her jaw. Her mouth was soft and yielding, as sweet as honey and twice as tempting. He slipped his hand beneath her tank top, aching to touch her. His fingers brushed her breast and instantly the nipple rose taut.

His breath caught at her quick jerk of reaction. Unbearably aroused, he trailed his lips along the silky skin from her sharp cheekbones to her temple.

Leaning his brow against hers he closed his eyes and swallowed hard.

He had to bring himself back. In a minute he'd be trembling. Somehow this feisty woman always managed to tie him completely in knots.

He wanted nothing more at the moment than to make love to her. But he knew that he couldn't. Mustn't.

Because it wouldn't be fair to her. He'd seen the way she looked at him at times when she didn't think he was aware. Like last night, in the boat on the way home.

For heaven's sake, he'd been in love before, had had women who loved him in turn. Naturally he'd recognized that yearning look in Rebel's eyes for what it was.

If he cared for her, he'd go no further.

If he cared for her, he'd return her heart intact before she even had the chance to place it into his careless safekeeping.

Because that was exactly how he would accept her love: carelessly. Not that he was an unfeeling man, but simply because of who he was, the way things were. The *Arabesque* would be ready to sail tomorrow evening. He'd stay in Marathon only long enough to arrange for her transport to Miami, where his uncle planned to have her picked up and sailed over to the Bahamas. Then he'd be on the very next flight for Providence. Once he left the Keys he knew with certainty that he'd not be back.

So he lifted his head and ended the kiss. Because he did care. Because he didn't want Rebel falling in love with him. She deserved far better than that.

Besides, he was honest enough with himself to know that if he didn't stop right now, he'd end up making love to her inspite of the consequences. In spite of everything. She was just too desirable, this fisherman's daughter.

For a long time both of them sat in silence, not looking at each other. The sun beat down from a cloudless sky. Out on the water, the seagulls wheeled and screamed. Josh knew he had to say something. To let her know how he felt without hurting her. He cleared his throat.

"Rebel—"

But she'd managed to guess his thoughts from the moment he'd lifted his mouth away from hers, knew his intent even before he dropped his hands to his sides. Amazing, how quickly he could withdraw into himself so that passion and promise no longer sizzled between them.

"You don't have to say anything. It's okay."

"But—"

She leaned over to lay a finger against his lips and was surprised that she wasn't trembling, that she could look calmly into his dark, serious eyes. "It's okay. Really."

But of course it wasn't. She'd never dreamed that rejection could hurt so much. That it could batter her heart until it lay like some awful, wounded weight inside her.

Josh didn't want her. He had his reasons, and she knew them all. Understood them, even. But still it hurt. Worse than she'd imagined.

On the other hand, she'd danced in and out of bad situations often enough in her life to remember to shake it off and smile. Never let anyone else catch on.

Boldly she slipped her arms around Josh's neck and brushed his lips with hers. "It's really, truly all right." She kept her voice light, teasing. "Now, how about lunch? I'm starving."

Chapter Seven

Lee was waiting for them at the dock when they returned. Rebel cut the motor and tossed him the line. "What are you doing home so early? Don't tell me somebody won the tournament!"

"Rebel, it's Pop."

She looked up, her smile fading. "What do you mean?"

"He's gone over to the Doughertys'. We had trouble on the water."

"Uh-oh."

"I been trying to get you on the radio." Lee's freckled face was pale. Josh didn't have to be told that he was scared.

Rebel slowly put down the pack she'd slung over her shoulder. "How long has he been gone?"

"An hour, maybe more. I don't know."

"Okay. I'm on my way." She climbed into the back of the skiff. "Cast us off, would you?"

Josh stopped her with a hand on her arm as she tried to restart the motor. "What's going on?"

"Pop's gone over to Marathon to pick a fight with the Dougherty brothers."

"The ones you told me run a rival fishing charter? What for?"

"That's what I'm going to find out." Rebel's voice was hard.

Josh whipped around to confront the boy. "Lee, what happened while you and your dad were fishing today?"

"Nothing until Mr. Jennings hooked a sailfish. The minute we saw it break water we could tell it was a winner. The biggest one yet. Right away Pop started braggin' on the radio—"

"Naturally," Rebel said between clenched teeth.

"—and the Doughertys overheard. They weren't but a mile away, probably over that reef wreck near Pop's favorite grouper hole. Well, they came flyin' over and ran across our wake."

"Let me guess." Rebel's eyes were bright with fury. "While coming to get a closer look, they just happened to cut the line with their propeller. Mr. Jennings's catch got away. Of course they called Pop on the radio right away to apologize. Said it was an accident."

Lee nodded miserably.

Josh still hadn't let go of Rebel's arm. Now he tightened his grip to get her attention. "Has this happened before?"

She nodded without looking at him. He could tell she was itching to shake him off and start the motor. "Pop said the next time it happened he was going to take care of them good." Her head came up. Her angry gaze seared his. "There are three of them, Josh. They hate Pop as much as he hates them. They're big, too. And mean."

"Then he should have called the police."

"To tell them what?" Rebel's tone was scornful. "The Doughertys haven't committed any crime. All they did was run over Pop's fishing line. Big deal. It happens a lot. What can he prove?"

"But if he told them—"

"Besides," Rebel interrupted stubbornly, "that's not the way things are done around here. Now would you please let me go?"

"Why? So you can go after him? Fight them yourself?"

"Josh, let me go."

"No."

"It's none of your business."

Damn it, yes, it was. He wasn't about to let her take off half-cocked, the way her crazy father had. What was she going to do once she caught up with the Doughertys, anyway? Put them in a headlock the way she had him?

Lee's voice came from the dock, all thin and

wobbly with unshed tears. "I been waiting and waiting for you to get back. Rebel, please, will you do something? You gotta help Pop!"

"I will as soon as this…this gorilla lets me go."

Grabbing her by the upper arms, Josh hauled her to her feet. She stood with her chin tipped, glaring up at him, as scrappy as ever, but certainly no match for three homegrown men out to cause trouble.

Good luck telling her that, Josh thought, exasperated. He took a deep breath. "Rebel, listen. I'll let you go, but only if you promise to let me handle this."

Her eyes widened. "You mean you'll come with me?"

"No, because you're not going at all. Okay, okay," he amended as he saw the mutiny creep into her expression. "You might as well show me where they live. But that's as far as it goes, got that? The rest you leave up to me."

"I'm not about to—"

"Is that clear?"

There was something in his eyes that made Rebel bite back her words and slowly nod her head. Something hard and ruthless, even dangerous. A side of Josh she hadn't known existed. A side that surprised her and made her wonder about the man beneath that easygoing nature. She was suddenly aware of the barely leashed strength in the fingers that gripped her arms. Remembered despite herself

corners of her mind. What if he was wrong? There were three of them, and they certainly hadn't honed their muscles the way Josh had by working out in an exclusive health club. These were hardened seamen, used to hauling in enormous fish and carrying heavy equipment to and from the water.

"Rebel." Josh was watching her intently. "I said it was going to be okay. I wish you'd believe that."

"I'm trying real hard."

Leaning down, he smoothed the frown line from between her eyes with a gentle forefinger. "Trust me." His voice was low, husky. She could feel it shivering through her like a caress. "Please."

"You make it sound so easy."

"Because it is. Your father may be impulsive, but he isn't a fool. He'll listen to reason."

"Provided we get there in time."

"We will." He refused to believe otherwise.

"What about the Doughertys?"

"What about them?"

"How will you handle them if they, you know—"

"Get ugly?"

She nodded, her eyes wide, her face pale.

"Sweetheart, in my profession I eat guys like that for breakfast." He leaned back when she smiled. "That's better."

"Josh, I know what you're doing."

"What?"

"You're being cheerful on purpose."

"How can you say that? I'm always cheerful."

"You're only pretending so I'll feel better."

"Rebel, you wound me. I *never* pretend. Besides, how can I be putting you on? How can anyone *not* feel cheerful with a sunset like this?"

"Huh?"

"Remember when the *Arabesque* ran aground? How all of us were so upset? Except you. You made me look at the night sky, showed me how beautiful it was. Called me an idiot for not seeing anything beyond my annoyance."

She looked at him wonderingly. "I can't believe you remember that."

"Honey, I remember every little thing you've ever said to me. Now, please take a look, will you?"

Rebel did, her heart so full of gratitude that she thought it might burst. In that moment she believed him capable of anything.

To be honest, the sunset *was* spectacular. A three-hundred-sixty-degree panorama of flaming orange, lavender and pink. The colors reflected on the placid bay were as vivid as those in the wide sky above. The skiff churned out a golden wake as it sped through the glowing water. Josh's chestnut curls were touched with fire.

Sure enough, Rebel could feel herself relaxing. "You're right. There's nothing like a sunset in the Keys."

Pleased that some of the fear had eased from her

face, he squeezed her shoulder. A simple, reassuring gesture. Then his hand brushed upward to curl around her neck, his fingers tangling in her short, silky hair, his thumb stroking the pulse at the curve of her jaw. Not reassuring at all. Very disturbing, very sensual.

"You'll have to take me to Key West sometime. I understand sunset is something to celebrate down there."

Rebel wanted to melt into his caress. She did her best to resist the pull of their bodies, the shivering scrape that was Josh's husky voice against her nerves. "For sure. Nobody 'does' the sunset like a conch."

"What's a conch?"

She sat up, if only to make his hand slide away. She mustn't let him affect her like this. "That's what we call people who've lived there all their lives."

"Funny, but I always have to remind myself that the Keys are part of the US of A. You people seem to have your own way of life, your own language, and you do things so differently down here."

"It's a zany place."

And you're one wonderfully zany woman, Josh thought. One who does zany things to me. Who makes me want to kiss you when I know I shouldn't. Touch you when I know it will only lead to trouble.

He was still trying to get over the effect she'd

had on him when he'd curled his hand around her neck. For a moment he'd been convinced that she was going to melt against him, and had felt anticipation rush like heat through his blood. When she'd moved away instead, she'd taken the warmth with her. He told himself he didn't care.

Up ahead, a boat came roaring from between the docks of the marina. Cutting a wide arc around a channel marker, it bore down on them at full throttle.

Rebel's breath caught. "It's Pop!"

"You sure?"

She snorted. "I can recognize his boat, can't I?"

He took no offense at her biting retort. He knew how worried she was.

Pop cut the engine as he neared, and the skiff quickly pulled alongside. He was sitting at the wheel, a cigar in its customary place between scowling lips. Rebel, scanning his face anxiously for signs of bruises, swelling or cuts in need of stitching felt her jaw dropping.

"Pop! You're okay!"

"Why shouldn't I be?" His voice sounded the same, except for its customary growl. It wasn't there. Rebel's smile faded.

"Pop, what's wrong?"

She had risen to her feet as she spoke, but Josh was ahead of her. He'd already noticed the older man's pallid skin and the beads of sweat dotting his brow.

"Rebel, tie up." Stepping across the gap onto the other boat, he put a hand on Pop's shoulder. "Time to come clean. What did they do to you?"

"Nothin'. We traded insults, that's all."

Josh had been feeling Pop's pulse without the old man knowing it. His heartbeat was racing, thready. Josh's eyes narrowed. "You'd better tell me what happened."

"I said there ain't nothin' to tell! Never laid a hand on any of 'em, and neither did they! I didn't so much as set foot on their blasted dock. Just talked to 'em from my boat. Now, would you kindly quit all this fussin'?" He jerked his shoulder to bump Josh's hand away, then inhaled sharply.

"What's hurting, Pop?" Josh asked gently.

Pop's head fell forward. His eyes closed. "M'leg."

Rebel, who had scrambled on board after securing the skiff, froze at his words. Her hands flew to her cheeks. "Pop! They didn't shoot you, did they?"

"No, they didn't shoot me! For cryin' out loud!"

Josh had gone down on one knee and was rolling up Pop's pant leg. Watching the older man's face, he probed with gentle fingers. Pop gasped and went white when Josh touched his shin.

"Broken, ain't it?" he wheezed.

"I'm afraid so. Lucky for you it's not a compound fracture. How'd it happen?"

Pop's face reddened. "I slipped!" he yelled.

"Can you believe it? On the dock, right in front of those brain-dead SOBs! 'Course there was no sense in bashin' their heads in after that! It was all I could do to get back to my boat without them knowin'!"

Behind him Rebel had gone pale. Josh spoke to her commandingly, tucking away the desire to comfort in another part of his brain. There was no time for that now. "Rebel, clear a place where your father can lie down. We've got to immobilize his leg."

"How do we do that?" she asked in a whisper.

Josh opened one of the tackle boxes and took out a knife. Calmly, expertly, he cut away Pop's pant leg. "Just leave that to me. Meantime, I want you to get us to the marina as fast as you can. Radio ahead for an ambulance. Where's the nearest hospital?"

"Hospital?" Pop jerked upright. "Ain't no way in the world—" But he collapsed with a groan the moment he tried to put weight on his injured leg.

Josh caught the old man and lowered him gently to the deck. His calm, steadying gaze found Rebel's. "Come on, honey. Let's go."

It seemed like hours before they let Rebel in to see her father. She had to wait through admissions, X rays and the excruciating task of setting a badly broken bone while the emergency-room staff flitted in and out and refused to answer her questions.

"Wait for the doctor," they kept saying until she thought she'd scream.

She wished she didn't feel so alone. Maybe she'd been too impulsive when she'd insisted that Josh didn't have to wait here with her. Heaven knows she needed him now.

Just when she was ready to demand to see the doctor, the doors whispered open.

"Ms. McCade? This way, please."

They'd given Pop a semiprivate room, but before Rebel could start feeling sorry for his roommate she was informed that Pop was the only patient on the floor. As she tiptoed inside, she thought he looked awfully strange, lying in a hospital bed wearing an ill-fitting hospital gown, with his leg all done up in plaster. Naturally he was scowling and acting thoroughly peevish.

"Nurse gave me painkillers, but they ain't workin'."

"Should've given you mood killers instead." Rebel bent to kiss his cheek. "Then again, the strength they'd have to give you to improve your mood would probably be toxic."

"Ha, ha. Get me a cigar, will you, kid?"

"No."

Pop muttered something beneath his breath, but Rebel wasn't fooled. He was weak and in pain, not his tough old self. Still, she knew better than to let on. Perching on the edge of his bed, taking care not to jostle his broken leg, she cast about for a way to distract him.

"I talked to Lee a little while ago. He sounded pretty upset on the phone. Will you call him in the morning? Let him know you're okay?"

"Why should I? I'll be home tonight."

"No, Pop."

"I'm not spending the night here, Reb."

"Yes, you are. And tomorrow night, too, if they say so."

"Bah."

"Pop, the tournament's over. It ended today. I'm driving everybody to the airport tomorrow. You might as well rest up until the new guests arrive. Besides, there's always next year."

"Don't know if there will be or not. Never seen the boys so mad before. 'Specially Harp. Fit to bust a blood vessel when that fish got away. He won't be comin' back to McCades' again."

"Boy, you really are feeling sorry for yourself, aren't you?"

Pop flapped a hand toward the cast on his leg. "Well, ain't I got the right?"

"Yes, you certainly do. But that's as far as it goes. No whining about how your life is completely ruined."

"I raised me a heartless girl."

"That you did. Listen, I'm on my way home. It's late and I still have to fix dinner." She could tell he was tired, but Heaven help her if she let him think she was leaving for his sake. "Lee won't rest until I tell him face-to-face that you're going to live. And somebody has to break the news to Monster."

At least that brought a smile to his face. After a moment Pop sighed and tugged at the collar of his hospital gown. Tried to look as if he didn't mind being abandoned. "By the way, where's Alden?"

"I sent him home in the skiff before it got too dark."

"Guess I owe him one. The paramedics said he did all the right things."

"I'm glad he was there, Pop." Rebel stooped to kiss his cheek in farewell.

He caught her wrist and looked at her. "When's he leaving?"

"Tomorrow, I guess. I was going to ask if he wanted to catch a ride to the airport with the others."

"There's a marlin tournament starts tomorrow."

"So?"

"Alden might like to give it a whirl."

"Go to sleep, Pop. You're delirious."

"He's a natural."

"But he doesn't like to fish. He told me so."

Pop pursed his lips. "Too bad."

"Besides, you hate that tournament."

"I know. I been tellin' that club for years there ain't no sense wastin' time on marlin till March. They don't listen. Nobody does." He snorted.

"Weekenders. Think they know everythin' about the sport. Don't know bull, do they?"

"No."

He looked at her keenly, still holding her wrist. "So what's eating you? Besides all this fuss about my leg, I mean?"

"Nothing. I'm fine."

"The hell you are. I know you, Reb. What's on your mind?"

She couldn't help herself. She just had to tell somebody how she felt. It might as well be Pop. "I've never been so miserable, Pop. I think I'm falling in love with him."

"Oh." Silence. "That's too bad."

"Yeah, I know."

More silence.

"Serious, is it?"

"For me? I guess so. Maybe."

He sighed. "Couldn't have set your heart on some local fella, huh?"

Rebel snorted, the sound an exact replica of his. "No need to look so worried, Pop. You know darned well this'll never go anywhere. It's not as though he's taking me back to Rhode Island or anything. What a joke that'd be! Could you see me entertaining his business partners? Giving dinner parties in a fancy dress?"

"If you cooked 'em, yeah."

"Oh, Pop."

"Sorry, hon. I know what you mean. He ain't exactly interested in a Florida girl, huh?"

She drew a shaky breath and said, "No," in a small, miserable voice.

"Hurts, don't it?"

She bit her lip and nodded without speaking.

"I felt that way when your mother left, you know. Tried my best to keep her happy, year after year, but it never worked out. She didn't belong here. The Keys were never the right place for her. Took both of us a long time to figure that out. Young and dumb, you know how it is. Besides, we are what we are, Reb. No sense in tryin' to change that."

"I know."

"Or be ashamed of it, neither."

"Who's ashamed? Did I say I was ashamed?"

"No, you didn't. Put down your dukes, kid. I'm on your side, remember?"

"Okay." Rebel slung her bag over her shoulder. "Try to sleep. I'll stop in on my way back from the airport tomorrow. In the meantime, do what the nurses tell you or else. No sneaking out to the convenience store for a smoke."

"No, ma'am."

"I mean it, Pop."

"Bah."

"I love you."

"I know. You can't help yourself."

What was a daughter supposed to do with a father like Pop? Rebel stopped at the nurses' station on the way out to give them a few kindly words of warning. They assured her, laughing, that since everyone on staff was familiar with Captain Pop McCade she had nothing to worry about. Rebel wasn't sure if she should laugh with them or hire a security guard to stand outside his door, anyway.

She had followed the ambulance to the hospital in Pop's beat-up Buick. Now, driving back to the marina, she tried to sort out her emotions. It was impossible. There were just too many, all of them fighting inside her for dominance. And she was tired, too. Exhausted. As though Pop's accident and the voicing of her feelings about Josh had drained her completely.

Tomorrow. She'd feel better tomorrow, after a good night's sleep and with some distance between herself and the events of today.

But tomorrow Josh could well be leaving.

When she got to the marina she found some of the folks still waiting around for her, wanting an update on Pop's condition. Touched, Rebel spent a few minutes chatting with them, then took the boat home.

Cutting the engine when she reached Gasparilla's familiar cove, she drifted toward the dock. Through the trees she could see that the lights were on in Josh's cottage. For a moment she was tempted to knock on his door, crawl into his lap when he opened it and lay her aching head on his strong, comforting shoulder.

She really must be tired. Fatigue was making her lose her sanity.

Scowling, she reached over to grab a piling and tied up the boat. Yellow Dog ran back and forth on the dock above, whining. Stepping across the gap between them, she stooped to fondle his ears. "It's okay, guy. Pop's gonna be fine."

"That's exactly what we wanted to hear."

Rebel looked up. All of them, Lee, Josh and Pop's four clients, were coming through the darkness toward her.

"Was he okay, Reb, really?"

She ruffled her brother's hair, which she knew he hated, only because she didn't know how else to comfort him. Tears stung her eyes when he actually cuddled against her hand. Apparently Pop's accident had unsettled both of them badly.

"Reb? How is he?"

She kept her tone light. "The whole time I was with him he was growling and carrying on and nagging me for a cigar."

"He'll live," Harp and Ted decided in unison.

All of them laughed. Lee tugged at her hand. "We kept supper for you, Reb. Mr. Jennings fixed burgers on the grill, and Mr. Walsh made potato salad."

She scanned their smiling faces wonderingly. "You're kidding."

"No, honestly. Josh even cooked macaroni 'n cheese." The way Lee was looking at Josh made it clear that he had found a new hero. Not only because Josh had helped save Pop, but because macaroni and cheese was Lee's all-round favorite food and Rebel stubbornly refused to serve it whenever they had guests.

Now she looked at Josh, too, for the first time since returning home. Not that she hadn't been aware of him. Her whole being seemed to hum whenever he was near. She wanted to thank him— for so much. But not here, not in front of the others. She'd only embarrass herself by getting emotional. She'd always hated tears.

"So," she said instead, striving to sound cheerful, "when do we eat?"

Harp stepped aside with a flourish and a bow. "Right this minute, if you like. This way, please, madame."

The Doughertys were the main topic at the dinner table. So was the trophy fish they had made Harp lose.

"Absolutely no problem," he announced much to Rebel's surprise. "I'm not giving up."

"But the tournament's over," she reminded him.

"I know it is, but we've been talking, and we all agreed that somebody has to stay and take another shot. The Tamarind Sportsmen Club Invitational starts Tuesday, doesn't it?"

"Well, yes, but none of you have ever—"

"Rebel, we've been coming here every February for the past fifteen years. We've entered the Pro-Max Tournament every year since then, and we've never come closer to winning than today. You don't really expect us to go home as if nothing happened?"

Actually, she did. In the past, their busy lives had prevented them from overstaying so much as a single day. Their complaints about their lack of vacation time had always been vocal, but none of them had ever done anything about it.

"Three days," Harp said quietly. "I'm giving it another three days. You got folks coming?"

"Not until Thursday. Permit and red drum anglers."

"Good. I'll stay in number two till then, then move up to the house, if that's okay with you and your father. Tuesday morning, you're taking me out after marlin. We're gonna beat the Doughertys this time, and win the Invitational to boot."

There were murmurs of assent from the others. Rebel shook her head. "Let me get this straight. You want *me* to captain Pop's boat while he's in the hospital? But I don't know the least thing about winning a tournament!"

"Don't sell yourself short, Reb. How long have you been crewing for him? Since you were Lee's age? Longer?"

"I guess."

"So, you're bound to have absorbed enough to make a go of it on your own."

"I'm not sure about that. You know this isn't the best season for marlin."

"Reb, don't tell me you're scared."

"Umm…"

"Where's your sense of adventure?"

"You don't miss a trick, do you, Harp?" But she was smiling a little.

"There, you see? So what's the worry?"

Her smile became wry. "Only everything."

"Come on. You can always ask for advice, can't you?" Ted Walsh insisted.

Lee nodded eagerly. "That's right, Reb! I was thinkin' we could patch our radio through to Pop's hospital room. Then he could give us ship-to-shore advice!"

"Us?"

He puffed out his chest. "I'm deckhand whenever I'm not in school, right?"

"Well, yes, but… Oh, man, I don't know about this." She brightened suddenly. "You're all forgetting something. We're still one person short."

"No, you're not." Josh spoke for the first time. "I'm coming, too."

Rebel swiveled to stare at him. "But you're leaving tomorrow. Your uncle's boat—"

"It's settled, Rebel," Ted Walsh interrupted firmly. "Don't try to talk him or Harp out of it. The rest of us would stay if we could, but at least this way somebody's got another chance.''

''Damned right,'' the others muttered.

Looking at their set faces, Rebel could understand how they felt. Pop's services didn't come cheap. A lot of money had been riding on that tournament; a lot of money had been lost thanks to the Doughertys' dirty trick. She couldn't really blame them for wanting revenge.

''So, are you free for the next few days?'' Harp demanded.

''Well, to be honest, I've lined up some work over at Stokes' Marina—''

''Those are dry-docked boats,'' Lee said quickly. ''They can wait a couple days, can't they?''

Actually, they could. And Josh would be staying....

But Josh hated fishing. Hated being away from his office. Why, then, had he decided to help out?

For Harp's sake, not hers.

Rebel looked around at their expectant faces. Nobody was smiling. The matter was pretty serious, after all.

She sighed. ''Okay. I suppose you can count me in.''

''All right!'' Whooping, Lee punched his fists in the air.

Only Josh lingered after the group broke up. Leaning against the kitchen counter, he smiled at her. ''You're one special lady, you know that?''

Absurdly, tears stung her eyes. Did he really think so? She tossed her head, afraid of letting him see how much his words moved her. "I try."

For a moment she could have sworn that he looked disappointed at her reaction. But then he shrugged and started for the door. "Guess I'd better get my gear together."

He didn't wait to hear her reply. The screen door slammed and Rebel was alone.

Chapter Eight

"I've been meaning to ask you something."

Josh put down the cooler he was carrying. "What?"

"How did you know what to do? With Pop, I mean? You must have some sort of medical training." Rebel was loading gear into the boat as she spoke. It was late, long after dinner, but the moon was full. Bright enough to shed silver light on the water and the dock. Cicadas shrilled in the treetops. A night bird called on the tidal flats.

"As a matter of fact, I do."

"What kind? Red Cross? CPR?"

"Actually, I went to medical school for a while."

"Really? How long?"

"Um, eight years."

She blinked. "But—but that's long enough to have graduated!"

"I did."

"From where?"

"Johns Hopkins."

"Johns—" Her voice trailed off in disbelief. "Josh! With a *degree?*"

He nodded without looking at her.

"I don't understand. What—"

"Can we talk about something else, Rebel?"

"No." She jumped from the boat down to the dock and peered challengingly into his face. "You're telling me you have a medical degree, a legitimate one, which you're obviously not putting to use. You don't want to talk about it, which makes me think there's some kind of problem here. I don't mean to pry—"

"Well, you are."

She ignored that. She was too stunned by what she'd heard. "Why, Josh?"

He looked into her upturned face, his mouth a tight line. She really had no qualms about going right for the throat, did she? But he couldn't be angry with her. She was just being Rebel. He was starting to believe nothing she could say or do would ever make him angry.

"Josh, please."

"Okay. I'll give you the basics if you promise to leave me alone."

Rebel nodded, very solemn.

"I'd always wanted to study medicine, even as a kid." Hefting the cooler, he stepped into the stern of the boat. "I applied to Johns Hopkins after finishing my undergraduate work at Harvard. To make a long story short, after passing my boards I went into practice with an old family friend, a cardiologist in New Hampshire. Then my father suffered a stroke. Since there was no one he trusted to take over the business, I stepped in to fill his shoes."

"Just like that?"

"Just like that."

She glared at his back. "I find that hard to believe."

"Rebel, I didn't mind."

"I'm talking about the fact that he didn't have anyone to take his place. You were his only child?"

"The one and only."

"So he must have realized when you entered medical school that you wouldn't be available to take over when he retired, whether he had a stroke or not. He must have been grooming *some*body!"

Josh scowled at her, feeling the anger of too many old wounds rising to the surface. "You're not dumb, are you?"

"For a hick, no," she retorted, annoyed. Not at him. At his father. "You're telling me there was no one else—"

"The Alden Foundation's been run by a member of my family since its inception three generations ago. My father was always hoping I'd have a change of heart, that I'd lose interest in medicine after a taste of private practice. That's why he wasn't 'grooming' anyone else. When he had that stroke, I agreed to step in temporarily. He never had the chance to appoint someone to take my place. He died a few months later."

"Josh, I'm sorry."

That was Rebel for you, he thought wryly. One minute she was out to murder somebody, the next she was expressing genuine sorrow at that same person's death.

"My mother was devastated when he died. I couldn't heap more heartache on her."

"They'd had a happy marriage?"

Josh nodded.

Rebel frowned at him. He could almost see the gears working as she tried to come up with a way to make things right again.

He was touched, even though he knew there was no sense in it. She could never come up with anything he himself hadn't tried, long ago, before he'd had to bury hope beneath duty and obligation. Besides, he no longer minded. The foundation made a sweeping difference in countless lives—far more than a simple physician could ever hope to.

He opened his mouth to tell her as much, to make her understand why he'd made his decision and why he intended to abide by it, then as now. But she interrupted him, her eyes holding his.

"It's okay, Josh. You don't have to say anything else."

"Good." He secured the cooler, then started back for another load.

"Just one more question."

He sighed. "I should've known. Okay, shoot."

"Can't Reardon—"

"No, Reb. Don't even start. Reardon Tate holding forth in my boardroom is a disaster waiting to happen. I'd rather see your father in charge of the place."

Her nose wrinkled. "That bad?"

"Worse."

"But—"

Stepping down to the dock beside her, he put a finger to her lips. "No more questions. You promised."

So she had. But it was hard to keep quiet with so much going on inside her. Resentment, frustration, a fierce protectiveness—all squeezed her heart. She didn't think for a minute that Josh was as happy with his life as he made out to be. Not when she'd heard the way he sometimes talked about his work and the people in his office. Not when she'd seen how tense and irritable he'd been when he first came to the Keys.

And she couldn't help remembering how he'd acted with Pop when Pop got hurt, how gentle and reassuring he'd been. He probably hadn't even been aware of the change in him. A wonderful change, not like that ruthless CEO person who'd popped up when the situation with the Doughertys had threatened.

Her heart ached with a hopeless, helpless love for him. Oh, Josh, you don't even know, do you?

Sure, he did. He must. But it wasn't fair to call him onto the floor like this. To open old wounds and accuse him of something she didn't really understand.

"Josh—"

He rounded on her, shaking his head, and the look in his eyes made her clamp her mouth shut. If she loved him, which she did, she'd accept him for what he was. What he did. But only if he was being honest with himself. And she wasn't exactly sure that he was.

They finished loading in silence, then walked up the path to his cottage without speaking. Rebel told him good-night and started toward the house. "I'll see you at four. Need a wake-up call?"

"No." Josh paused with his hand on the door latch. "Rebel?"

She turned on the path.

"I don't mind doing what I do. Really. I want you to believe that."

She fisted a hand on her hip. "Are you trying to convince me, Josh Alden, or yourself?"

He glowered at her. "Please don't start that again."

"I'm not. I didn't say a word. You're the one who started it this time."

"Because I want you to let it go, Rebel. I know you. You'll hound me to death if you think—"

"*Hound* you!" She could feel her hackles rising and was glad of it. She'd been spoiling for a fight ever since they'd started loading the boat. "I don't intend to give you any trouble, Mr. Alden! If something's naggin' at you, it's your conscience, not me."

He strode up the path toward her, furious now. "So you think I'm not happy with what I do? That I'd rather be practicing medicine, that I've been denying the truth to myself all these years?" He halted in front of her, scorching her with the heat of his anger. "Since when do you know so much about me, anyway?"

Since I've fallen in love with you. Since I've come to understand something of the workings of your heart. Since I feel things about you that other people might miss altogether.

She opened her mouth just as Josh jabbed a finger at the tip of her nose. "No answer for once, Rebel? Good. Let's keep it that way. Because you've got no right to poke that cute little nose of yours where it has no business being. My life, and what I choose to do with it, is no concern of yours."

She ignored his waving finger. "How come you're so mad, Josh?"

"I'm not mad!"

"Pop never gets mad at me either, unless I've hit him where it counts."

She was so unflappable, so darned...cute that his temper erupted. "So you've gone ahead and analyzed and judged and condemned me all in the space of a single half hour, have you? Decided you know more about me than me or my family? Sorry, but you don't know a damned thing, Scarlett Elizabeth McCade. You can't possibly understand my personal affairs. You have no idea what goes on at Alden-Moore or how to manage a foundation! How can you? You run a fish camp, for cripes sake!"

The words were out before he even knew he was going to say them. They quivered between them, hurtful, unfair, impossible to take back.

Rebel's hand dropped away from her hip as she straightened. Her voice was calm, her eyes were dry, even though her heart was weeping. "You're right. I guess I don't know a blessed thing. I'm as ignorant as folks come down here in the South."

Wheeling, she ran for the house. She had no idea if he called after her or not because her heart was hammering so loudly in her ears. Slamming through the house she stormed up the stairs to her room, closed the door and locked it.

Sitting down on the bed she drew her knees to her chin. She wasn't going to cry, damn it!

There was a knock on the door. "Reb?"

She closed her eyes for a moment. "It's late, Lee. Why aren't you in bed?"

"I was. But you made so much noise coming in. I thought..." He broke off. "It's hard talkin' through wood, Reb. Would you please open the door?"

She did so, propping a hand on her hip as she stood aside to let him in.

"Hoo, boy," he said when he saw her.

"What?"

"You're doing that thing."

"What thing?"

He copied her stance. "That thing you do, the way you stand whenever you're mad. Like you're just darin' somebody to take a poke at you."

She held up her fists. "Yeah? Wanna try?"

Lee grinned. "Nah. I don't pick fights with girls."

"Why, you—" She grabbed him in a headlock and rapped her knuckles against his skull.

When she let him go he collapsed on her bed, still grinning. "Feel better?"

She considered. "Matter of fact, I do."

"So what's wrong with you? Did you have a fight with your boyfriend?"

Her smile faded. She tossed her head. "Josh Alden is not my boyfriend."

"Coulda fooled me."

She punched his arm. "What's that supposed to mean?"

"I'm not dumb, Reb. I seen the way you look at him."

She suddenly developed a deep interest in the items on her dresser. "Yeah?"

He snickered. "Yeah. Enough to make ya sick." In the mirror she watched him mimic several very exaggerated lovestruck expressions.

"Oh, come on! Not like that!"

"Like that. And worse."

Rebel plunked herself down beside him and sighed. "Man. That's great. If my kid brother can tell..."

"Don't worry. Nobody knows. Especially Mr. Alden. He's much too thick."

Rebel bristled. "What's that supposed to mean?"

"Only that he's exactly like Mr. Walsh and Mr. Jennings. Like all of them. Get them out on a boat on vacation and what do they do? Talk business."

"Does that include Josh?"

Lee rolled his eyes. "All day. When we took him out with Pop, I couldn't understand a word him and Mr. Jennings were saying. Never mind the fish they caught. Just work, work, work. What a bore!"

"That doesn't make him *thick*."

"Yeah? Well, if he wasn't, he'd surely notice those goo-goo eyes you make at him."

"I don't make...what?"

"Goo-goo eyes."

"Goo-goo eyes at him." She sighed again, soft and sorrowful. "Not anymore."

"Like I said, you guys had a fight."

"An argument. I tried to tell Josh he doesn't really like the kind of work he does. He told me it was none of my business and that I didn't know what I was talking about."

Lee looked disgusted. "Is that the kind of stuff you fight about? Man, I'm glad I don't have a girlfriend."

Rebel tried to smile but failed. Her heart still hurt too much.

"I don't even like girls."

She gave him a playful slap. "In a year or two they'll start to seem a whole lot more interesting, trust me."

Lee made another face. Then he said carefully, "Know what I think?"

"What?"

"Maybe it isn't your business. You're not married to the guy or anything like that."

No, she wasn't. And even though Lee was just a kid, his words carried enough wisdom to bring a flush of embarrassment to her cheeks. He was right, darn him. No matter what she believed about Josh, felt for him, she had no right to pry into his life or tell him how to run it. And tomorrow she was going to start making sure she remembered that.

But it was hard to spend the entire day with the man you loved in a crowded boat and pretend you weren't in love with him or that every time he looked at you or spoke to you your heart didn't squeeze with longing and hurt. Hard to remember that he was paying you money to take him fishing, nothing more, and that in a few short days he'd be gone.

At least she was able to keep busy at the wheel of the boat, following the tournament fleet out to deep water and paying attention to her instruments. As deckhand, Lee did most of the physical work, and most of the talking with Josh and Harp. In fact, Rebel rarely had to deal with them at all.

But still the hours dragged. The weather wasn't helping any, being overcast with a stiff southwesterly breeze, so that nobody seemed to be having much luck with trolling.

Around noontime she spoke on the radio with somebody at the Marathon marina, who relayed a phone call to the hospital to check on Pop. Word came back that he was acting ornery, which of course meant that he was doing well.

At four o'clock Harp decided to call it a day. They'd caught enough mahi mahi for supper, but that was all. No marlin worth writing home about. Everyone was in low spirits as the boat sped home.

"Does anybody mind an early supper?" Rebel asked. "I want to take Lee to visit Pop."

Nobody did.

The broiled mahi mahi was delicious, of course, but nobody talked much during the meal. Harp looked so discouraged that Rebel felt deeply sorry for him.

"Maybe you should go out with somebody else tomorrow."

He glared at her. "That's the dumbest thing you've ever said, hon."

"But I'm not—"

"Yes, you are. Much better than you think. Not another word, okay? Now you and Lee go on. Visit your dad. I'll do the dishes."

"No way! We couldn't possibly—"

"You can, and you will." A boardroom bark had entered Harp's voice. "What am I? A paying guest or a friend of long standing?"

"Well, both," Rebel admitted with the glimmer of a smile.

"Go on. Get out of here."

On the way upstairs Rebel paused by his chair to kiss the top of his head. "Thanks. You're the best."

Harp growled, but he was obviously pleased.

She reappeared a few minutes later with her hair neatly combed and a gray sweatshirt pulled over a pair of faded jeans. Rebel in jeans was something to savor, but Josh kept his eyes on his plate, the way he had for most of the meal. It was only when he heard the boat keys jangling as she took them off the hook by the back door that he looked up.

"Need me to go with you?"

Rebel shook her head, keeping her eyes averted.

"I appreciate the offer, but we can manage. Lee? Ready to go?"

The screen door slammed behind them. A boat motor spluttered, then droned away. In her cage near the dining table, Monster lifted her head to let out a deafening screech of protest, but an icy look from Harp made her turn her back in a huff.

"Gotta treat all the McCades that way," he told Josh with a grin. "If you give them an inch, they'll take a mile."

"You're fond of them."

"Hell, yes. Like family. Good-hearted folk. I think the world of 'em." An unmistakable note of warning had crept into his tone, but Josh looked away, refusing to rise to the bait, hoping Harp would let it go.

Not a chance.

"You having trouble with Rebel?"

Josh laid aside his fork. "Excuse me?"

"I thought we'd freeze out on the water today, what with the chill between you."

Josh leaned back, his mouth thinning. "Harp, is this going to get personal?"

The other man shook his head, too much the diplomat. "I've known her since she was a kid, that's all. I don't want to see her involved in any trouble."

Josh couldn't help it. His lips twitched. "There's always trouble whenever Rebel's around."

"She's a wild one, all right." Harp pushed back his chair and began stacking dishes. "Not surprising, considering she takes so much after her pop. Those teenage years weren't easy. At least college helped mellow her out some."

Josh's head came up. "Rebel went to college?"

"Didn't she tell you?"

"No." Actually she had, but Josh had never really paid attention. It hadn't mattered then, but it did now. A lot. "Where?"

"Northwestern, I think, and the University of Indiana."

"Indiana? What on earth took her way out there?"

"A scholarship."

"In what?"

The phone in the kitchen rang. Harp went to answer it. "McCades'." He turned. "Josh, for you. Somebody named Tate."

"I'll take it in the study."

The call took a while. Reardon had been instructed by his father to obtain a detailed report on the status of his sailboat. He also had numerous questions of his own, mostly pertaining to Rebel. Since Josh wasn't willing to talk about her to anyone, especially Reardon, he kept his replies short.

Reardon, never any good at picking up on the obvious, kept on with his rambling monologue until Josh finally cut him short. Afterward he was obliged to pay his respects to his aunt, who insisted on speaking to him, too. By the time he returned to the kitchen, Harper had cleaned up, switched off the lights and retired to his cottage.

Feeling restless and irritable, Josh wandered down to the dock, but Rebel's boat was still gone. The wind hadn't lessened and the air was chilly. Even Yellow Dog didn't seem too eager to wait around.

"Come on. You can room with me for a while."

Yellow Dog flopped down happily on the rug in Josh's cottage, while Josh settled himself in a worn-out armchair and unfolded the newspaper.

"Gonna be a long night."

The tip of Yellow Dog's tail tapped in agreement. Yawning hugely, he laid his head on the floor.

That was how Rebel found them when she entered Josh's cottage several hours later. She'd sent Lee up to bed and whistled for the dog, then started searching when he didn't show up. She heard him whimper as she passed by Josh's cottage, and since the door was slightly ajar she'd peeked inside.

She saw at once that Josh had fallen asleep in the chair. Lamplight glinted on his unguarded face. He looked surprisingly boyish with his features relaxed, his head tipped to one side, his long legs sprawled across the hassock.

She watched him for a minute, her heart aching. Why, oh, why had she been so stupid as to let herself fall in love with him? Not until he'd showed up in her life had she come to understand how a person who was neither lonely nor in anyway unhappy could suddenly feel so dissatisfied. Josh had made her aware of a need she didn't even know she had until he'd come along to fulfill it.

He was cool water, she a runaway fire. Would she crumble into ashes when he left? Probably not, but her heart just might.

"Rebel?"

He was up and out of the chair, coming toward her with that loose, easy stride of his. He smiled at her, too blurry from sleep to hide his pleasure. Or was that just her wistful imagination?

Blushing, she started backing out the door. "Sorry. Didn't mean to wake you. I just came for the dog."

"How's Pop?"

"Okay."

He slapped a hand on the door before she could bolt through it. "That's it? Just okay?"

"Actually bad-tempered, unpleasant and a royal pain."

"In other words, making a complete recovery."

A smile peeked out. "How'd you know?"

"When's he being discharged?"

"The doctor hasn't decided yet. Probably tomorrow."

"But we're going offshore tomorrow."

"Yeah, well, I was meaning to talk to Harp about that. If there's a chance Pop might be coming home…"

Josh remembered the way Harp had talked about the McCades at supper. "He'll understand."

Rebel was still edging toward the door and Josh was compelled to step in front of her to make her stop. "Rebel, wait a minute. We need to talk. I owe you an apology."

"No, you don't."

He caught her arm. He didn't look sleepy or relaxed anymore. "I said things last night that I shouldn't have. I was out of line."

"No, I was. You were absolutely right. You're none of my business."

She was staring at the buttons of his shirt as she spoke, so she didn't see him wince.

God, what was it about this woman that got to him time after time? How did she manage to slam a fist into his gut with no more than a single glance or word? He had no idea. He only knew he couldn't stand being at odds with her. Their avoidance in the boat today had been bad enough.

"That's not how I see it." His voice was rough. "I don't think you would have pursued the subject if you didn't care. You do, don't you?"

Her mouth was dry. Dear lord, he could send a woman spinning clear off her feet with merely the warm light kindling in his eyes.

She waved a hand, very casual. "Sure, I care about you, Josh."

But she couldn't pull it off. Not feeling the way

she did about him. Not uttering words that came straight from her heart.

She saw his eyes darken at her tone. Saw the smile fade from his lips while a watchful stillness settled over his big frame. She would have bolted out of the door then, but he was still standing in front of it.

"Rebel."

"What?"

"Please look at me."

She shook her head, still watching his shirt buttons.

With a finger beneath her chin he tipped her face up. "Nothing's easy with you, you know that? You won't let me tuck you into some nice, simple corner where I can forget about you if I want to. Deal with you when I'm ready. Anybody ever tell you you have all the finesse of a hurricane?"

"All the time." She tried to speak lightly, but her words came out on a trembling breath.

Slowly, oh so slowly, he slid his arms around her waist and drew her to him until they stood joined at the hips, the thighs, the center of their beings. The tips of her breasts pressed against his shirtfront. Her gaze clung to his dark, hooded eyes.

"Little hurricane," he whispered against her mouth. "Would you kiss me?"

She couldn't have resisted him if she tried. Mesmerized, she let him draw her closer, let his mouth take possession of hers in a dreamy kind of caress.

Her head tipped back and her lips opened beneath his.

Not a hurricane, but a warm breeze, as natural as breathing. A quiet sigh as she melted into it while he bent her back like a blade of grass, molding her to him. Tongues grazed, mated. Desire began to burn like heat wherever they touched. Fire spread. Everywhere.

"I should go," she whispered against his mouth.

Yes, she should.

He deepened the kiss.

She linked her arms around his neck. Turned into him, against his hard body. The snaps of their jeans chinked softly.

"Rebel—"

"Don't. Please don't. I'm leaving."

His blood was hammering, his senses swimming. He wanted her. Wanted her so much that he ached.

He drew a deep, tortured breath, then lifted his mouth from hers. He saw that her eyes were huge and unfocused, swimming with desire, like his own. Reaching up, he took her wrists, felt the racing pulse beneath his fingers. Watching her, he unwrapped them from around his neck.

Only one word, one more kiss—that was all it would take to have her in his arms again, to waltz with her those few feet to the bed, to ease her out of those tight jeans, that loose-fitting top. To bury himself in the warmth that was Rebel. The sparkle of sunshine, the play of light on azure water, that he'd come to think of whenever he thought of her.

But he wanted the choice to be hers. It had to be hers. He cared that much. More.

Closing his eyes, he leaned his chin against the fragrant softness of her hair. His voice was thick with effort. "If you think you should go, then you'd better."

She opened dazed eyes to look at him, feeling an ache in her heart because she knew the decision was already made. By her? By him? She wasn't sure. She couldn't think straight anymore.

His expression might be ravaged, but his eyes were beautifully gentle. "Good night."

Confused, grateful, weepy, she turned and slipped outside. Yellow Dog padded after her.

The room was silent. Uttering a groan, Josh leaned his head against the door.

Chapter Nine

"Mr. Alden?"

Josh pried open bleary eyes. Morning sunshine poured through the cottage door. Lee McCade was standing at the foot of his bed, grinning.

"Hey, kid. What's up?"

"Pop's been discharged. We're on our way to fetch him. Rebel wanted to know if you'd like to come. Pop sort of asked."

Josh groaned and scrubbed his hands across his face. "What time is it?"

"Almost ten."

The fog started clearing a little. "But I thought—weren't we going fishing?"

"Mr. Jennings went by himself. On Lou Breeding's boat."

"Who?"

"He's a neighbor. Helps Pop out every now and then."

Josh groaned again. It was too much information to digest so early.

"Rebel fixed coffee. Said to bring you some."

Josh's eyelids came up the rest of the way. He sniffed. The kid had brought a mug of java on a tray, along with sugar and cream and a thermos refill.

Rebel McCade, I just might end up falling in love with you, after all.

"Do I have time to shower?"

"I guess."

He did, in record time, gulping coffee as he dressed. Then he hurried down to the dock with his hair still damp. Rebel was in the larger of the two sportsfishermen, readying the cockpit for departure. She was wearing a skimpy summer dress, navy blue with white polka dots, that barely brushed the tops of her sexy knees. White deck shoes without socks drew attention to her slim, sunbrowned legs and made Josh look away quickly before his mouth could start to water.

Luckily she was completely focused on fetching Pop. Her manner was distracted when she greeted him. "I thought Pop'd be more comfortable on the bigger boat. What do you think? Will he need to lie down?"

"He'll probably bite your head off if you dare suggest as much."

She barely cracked a smile.

"We could always charter an air ambulance."

"Do you think we should?" she asked.

"Rebel." He took hold of her arms, just above the elbows. She straightened to look at him. "Don't worry so much. We'll get him home and into bed without a hitch."

This time she did smile, her eyes softening with gratitude. "I'm glad you're here. I don't know a thing about this nursing stuff."

"Piece of cake. Trust me."

She felt herself relaxing. Putting her trust in Josh had always come easy, especially when he talked like that, looked at her like that. She wanted to sigh in contentment and lay her head against him, just for a moment.

But she knew better. After last night, she knew better.

If only he wasn't so hard to resist, darn him. With the breeze ruffling his chestnut curls and his dark eyes intent on her face, he looked so good that she found it hard enough to breathe, let alone keep on staring at him calmly. He was still gripping her arms with his big, capable hands, stroking her skin in pleasurable little circles with his thumbs.

Rebel could feel herself starting to shiver. The pull of their bodies was impossible to ignore. She had to fight the growing need to lean into him, to lift her mouth for the kiss she yearned for.

Josh's grip tightened in response. He, too, felt the clamoring of their hearts, their bodies. Slowly, slowly, his head dipped toward hers.

"Hey!" Lee landed with a thump in the stern. "You guys gonna stand there moonin' at each other, or are we gonna fetch Pop?"

Rebel spun away, laughing, to slap at him playfully. "Go on. Get the motor started."

Now how on earth did she manage that? Josh wondered irritably. He was still feeling breathless while Rebel...Rebel was scooting into the captain's seat, skirt hiked over browned thighs, humming beneath her breath as though nothing at all were amiss. Either she was a terrific faker, or he'd misread completely the desire he'd just seen turning her blue eyes to smoke.

Not until they were well across the channel did he manage to settle into the seat beside her with an easy smile of his own. "Is it true your father asked me to come?"

Rebel didn't take her eyes from the markers ahead. "Sure did. I think he's nervous about going home."

"Will he be on crutches, Mr. Alden?" Lee asked.

"Josh. My name's Josh. And you can count on it."

When they got to the hospital, they found Pop

sitting by his bed in a wheelchair, his cast leg propped up in front of him. Rebel's heart squeezed because he looked so frail. As though he'd aged and shrunk before her very eyes.

But there was nothing wrong with his temper or his bark. "'Bout time you got here! Been hours since I called!"

"We had to get your room ready." Rebel's voice was soothing. "And the boat. I thought you'd be more comfortable in the '34."

"That's no excuse."

"Josh had to have his coffee," Lee piped up. "He's slow as molasses in the mornin'."

Pop glowered at Josh, who'd crossed over to shake hands with the doctor. "Coulda brought it with him."

"He did. A whole thermos. Know what I think? Rebel's picked herself a real mornin' wuss. Oww!" Lee rubbed his ear, which his sister had just twisted painfully.

Pop scowled at them. "Cut it out, you two. This is a hospital, remember?"

Rebel was only too glad to comply. Casting a discreet glance at Josh, she was relieved to see that he was still talking with Dr. Reed. They continued conversing while she gathered up Pop's things. She kept an eye on them while she zipped the overnight bag, struck by the way Josh's whole manner had changed the moment he'd started discussing Pop's chart.

Nobody notices how different he is but me. Not Pop, not Lee, probably not even Josh.

Why?

Because she was in love with him. Was attuned to every little nuance, every change in him.

Oh, yes, she was definitely in love. Big time. If she'd ever had reason to doubt her feelings, they'd been put permanently to rest last night when she'd crawled, aching and close to tears, into her bed. She'd never done anything harder in her life than walk away from Josh's door. Knowing he'd left that decision up to her had made it all the more difficult to bear.

But she'd made the right choice. She had to believe that. She'd already lost her heart. She wasn't going to make matters worse by losing everything else to him, as well.

"Rebel." Josh was waving some papers at her. "Dr. Reed's given me the discharge instructions. Do you want him to review them with you?"

She shook her head, too overwhelmed to speak.

"Fine. I'll explain later. Just sign the release forms."

The trip back to Gasparilla was hard on Pop. The wind had picked up and there was a good-size chop on the bay. Pop didn't utter a word of complaint, but he had to be in pain, with the boat bucking like a bronco over the waves. Josh sat beside him, talking encouragingly, although the roar of the motor drowned out what they were saying. At any rate

Rebel was intent on getting them home as fast as possible. Lee prowled the deck, pale and silent. Poor kid, Rebel thought. This was the first time in his life that he'd ever seen his father unwell.

At the dock Josh offered a strong shoulder for Pop to lean on. Lee kept Yellow Dog out from underfoot while Rebel led the way, carrying the overnight bag. Josh took Pop straight up to his room even though he wanted to stop in the kitchen for a beer.

"I ain't no invalid," he complained, but Josh ignored him and headed for the stairs. Out on the porch Monster screamed her rage at being ignored.

Pop kept right on fussing when Josh lowered him onto the bed, but Rebel noticed that he took all the pills Josh counted out for him. And in the end he did agree to rest, but only after Josh had propped his leg up just the way he liked it.

She grinned at them both, knowing better than to interfere. "I'll be in the kitchen."

She was peeling shrimp at the sink when Josh joined her a few minutes later. They exchanged weary smiles.

"That was exhausting."

"I know. I couldn't have done it without you, Josh."

"For once I think I agree."

"How about lunch? I'm making shrimp salad."

"That'd be—"

The phone rang.

"Josh, it's for you. The boat yard."

She went to the refrigerator and took out sour cream, dill and onions while he talked. She kept on dicing and chopping while he hung up and crossed to the sink. Reaching over her shoulder, he homed in on a succulent shrimp. Rebel slapped his hand away.

"Wait till lunch."

"I can't. I'll have to pass. The truck's coming at two to pick up the boat. I'd like to be there."

Rebel glanced at the oven clock. "Better hurry, then."

"I will. Save some for me, okay?" He gave her shoulders a quick squeeze from behind. "Thanks."

While he was gone, she cleaned the cottages, straightened the house, fed Lee his lunch and did her best to make Pop comfortable. When Lee was invited to spend the night with a friend, she arranged to see him off at the dock. After he was gone she wandered down to the little strip of beach, Yellow Dog at her heels.

She sat for a long time with her feet trailing in the water, thinking. Staring across the bay she went over everything that had happened since Josh had come into her life. Remembered every word, every look, and especially the way he'd handled Pop just now, an amazing accomplishment.

After a while, her mind made up, she went back into the house and picked up the phone.

* * *

Josh didn't get back until suppertime. By then Harp had made it home, too, and they listened sympathetically to his description of another lousy day on the water.

"Well," Rebel said bracingly when he was done, "this isn't the worst trip you've ever had."

"No, it's not. And there's always next year," Harp agreed.

"Then you're coming back?"

"Of course I am. We all are. Don't tell me you've started believing your father's predictions of gloom and doom?"

"I guess I have. Sorry."

"It's very catching if you don't watch out. What about you, Alden? Care to try your hand at billfishing next year?"

Josh had been caught unawares. He set aside his knife, then took his time wiping his mouth with his napkin before answering. "I'll have to give it some thought." He looked across the table at Rebel, who was buttering a biscuit, her head bowed. "By the way, I went to the travel agent on my way back from town. My flight leaves at eleven tomorrow."

She pursed her lips, considering. No one could possibly guess from her expression how much of a shock he had dealt her. "In that case we'll have to leave the house early. Before seven."

"No need for you to drive me to Miami. I've rented a car. It's down at the marina."

"Hey, that's great," Harp said. "You can give me a lift. My flight leaves at two."

Josh frowned. "That's quite a wait."

"I don't mind. I'm used to killing time in airports. Rebel, this way you can stay here and look after Pop. Make sure his leg mends perfectly. We're going to need him next year to win the Pro-Max."

"Right," she said, trying to smile, but her face felt funny, as though it had turned to stone.

Harp pushed back his chair. "Hope you don't mind, but I'm all done in. Getting up at 3:00 a.m. day after day isn't as easy as it used to be. I'm not a young man anymore."

"Go to bed, Grandpa," Rebel agreed. "Need a nightcap before you go?"

"No, thanks. I'm going to say so long to Pop, then put up my feet and read the paper. Hold all my calls after nine, okay?"

"Will do."

"See you folks in the morning."

"Six-thirty," Josh called after him. Stacking up the dishes, he carried them into the kitchen.

Rebel followed him with a stack of her own. "You don't have to do that, Josh."

"Sure I do. It's my last night here."

She wished he wouldn't put it that way.

They worked side by side amiably enough, but the strain was obvious even to Yellow Dog, who watched them moving from counter to sink to dishwasher with his head on his paws. If a dog could look worried, Yellow Dog took the cake.

They didn't talk very much, and whatever they said sounded stilted. Josh expressed regret that he'd not be able to say goodbye to Lee. Rebel promised to give him the boy's address.

"Great. That way I can write to him in Michigan." He seemed intent on scrubbing the frying pan. "Would you like to have mine?"

"Sure." What for? They were never going to see each other again.

She felt like a sleepwalker going through the motions of cleaning up. Of trying not to think or feel. Already the pain of his leaving was overwhelming, before he'd even left. What was she going to do with herself from now on? How was she going to get from one day to the next, put one foot in front of the other, when her heart was shattered?

"If you're ever in Providence—" He winced before the words were out. He'd never said anything that sounded so lame.

"I doubt it. But thanks." Her voice was as remote as her expression.

Lord, he hated this. Hated the way they were tiptoeing around each other, avoiding glances, hardly speaking, refusing to admit that saying goodbye was going to be so hard.

Not only for her, Josh realized suddenly. She must mean something to him, or he wouldn't be feeling this way. Come to think of it, he'd been feeling this way ever since the travel agent had laid that plane ticket on the counter in front of him.

Rebel said quietly, "I can finish up here. You've probably got some packing to do."

"I guess."

"Good night. Thanks for the help."

"Sure." He hung up the dish towel and started for the door. Abruptly he whirled and caught her from behind before she could return to the sink. Hands on her shoulders, he turned her to him, looking deeply into her eyes and wishing he had the means to make them smile again. "Rebel, I have to go. You know that, don't you?"

She nodded. Of course she did.

"But we still have tonight. Can I take you to Callahan's? Maybe a movie?"

Longing flickered in her eyes, but then she shook her head. "Thanks, really, but I need to stay here with Pop."

Yes, she did. He'd forgotten. No reason, then, to go on holding her like this. Her eyes were already staring past him, her lovely mouth set in a wobbly line. The fact that she was trying not to cry slammed through him like a giant fist. He dropped his hands from her shoulders and spun away. "I'm going for a walk."

"Fine." She blinked as the screen door slammed behind him.

Even though the sun had set hours ago, the night wasn't entirely dark. The moon had risen and the lights from Marathon brightened the sky. Josh had left a floor lamp shining in his cottage, but Harp's was dark. Apparently he'd made good on his threat to go to bed early.

Hands in his pockets, Josh walked down to the dock. The wind crooned through the sea grapes and made the boats creak at their moorings. Over the past few days he'd come to appreciate the silence of the Keys and the smell of the salt air, the subtle changing of the tides. But tonight he couldn't find any peace in the vast quiet.

The thought of Providence, still in the hard grip of winter, loomed like a nightmare. The responsibilities of work, which he'd managed to push into the background until now, crashed down on him, made worse by the fact that he'd have to pay for neglecting them so long.

On the other hand, he was used to working hard, and the chaos that no doubt awaited him on his return didn't really scare him. Not the way saying goodbye to Rebel did.

Maddening, difficult woman. Why couldn't the *Arabesque* have picked up someone else that day? Why Rebel McCade, of all the people in the Florida Keys? Because Rebel was the one person who wasn't going to let him tuck her into some nice, comfortable corner of his mind where her memory would dim over time.

Frowning, he stooped to pat Yellow Dog, who

stood quietly beside him. "Maybe I could come back. Every year, like Harp and the others."

Yellow Dog whined.

"I know. Bad idea."

A cold nose pressed against his knee. Josh let out an exasperated sigh.

"Look, I know what you're trying to tell me. It's not that I don't care, it's just that I can't afford to...oh, great. Now she's got me talking to the dog." What next? A political debate with Monster? What on earth was he going to do about that crazy woman?

"Josh!"

He whirled. Rebel was running toward him, her navy dress a dark blur against the white of the oyster-shell path. She looked ethereal, slimly beautiful, and just for a moment he let himself fantasize what she'd do when she caught up with him. His heartbeat quickened. He could almost feel her arms winding around his neck and the softness of her lips opening beneath his.

"Josh! Can you come? Pop's running a fever."

Instantly the heat drained from his blood. His mind became clear and cold, focused. "How high?"

"He wouldn't let me take it. Told me I was making too much of a fuss." She stopped in front of him, her breasts rising and falling as she struggled for air. "Could you give it a try? I thought maybe you'd have more luck. You did before."

He took her upturned face in his hands. Tried to pour all the reassurance she needed into his voice alone when he ached to take her into his arms. "Don't look so worried. An infection's not uncommon. That's why he's on antibiotics."

"But—".

"Shh. I'll look in on him to make sure."

She caught hold of his wrists to steady herself. "Thanks. You're pretty brave, you know that?"

A smile tugged at his mouth. Her ability to bounce back like this never failed to delight him. "Maybe you'd better wait here. He'll probably refuse to see me if he thinks you put me up to it."

"You're right. I didn't think of that."

But Josh had. As would any good doctor dealing with a difficult patient. Rebel longed to point out as much, but knew better. He wouldn't appreciate her telling him things he didn't want to hear. He'd only get surly, withdraw from her, and Lord knows she wasn't about to fight with him on his last night here.

His last night...

Her vision swam as she watched him disappear up the path.

She was sitting at the porch table, chin in hand, when he came back downstairs. The moment he said her name she bolted to her feet.

"Sweetheart, don't. Everything's fine."

"Does he have a fever?"

"The kind you'd expect with a low-grade infection, but it's truly nothing to worry about. He's asleep now."

"He is? How did you manage that?"

"I didn't have to do a thing. He's tired, Reb. It's been an exhausting day."

"I know, I know." She hugged herself with her arms. "I'm overreacting, but I'm just not used to him being hurt or sick or in bed or looking so...*old*." She turned away from him to swipe at her eyes. Lord, she was being emotional tonight! Josh's leaving had her all churned up.

"Rebel."

Oh, no, not that, too. She'd never been able to stand it when he said her name like that, so tender and sweet, as though he knew perfectly well that she was crying. Rebel wasn't used to tenderness. Lord knows Pop had always been as abrasive as sandpaper. Which probably explained why she simply melted inside at Josh's tone, why something seemed to give way in her heart so that the tears started flowing and she couldn't make them stop.

"Rebel, will you look at me?"

She shook her head.

"Come on. It's not a crime to cry."

"It is for me." Her voice was thick, wobbly. "I never cry. I hate crying."

"I know you do. And I said once that it should be a federal crime to make you sad. Remember?"

Of course she did. She remembered just about

every word he'd ever said to her. They were all she'd have left of him when he was gone. She could already picture herself taking them out to replay in her mind, over and over, in her lonely bed at night.

A sob caught in her throat. She couldn't believe she was actually having such self-pitying thoughts. Whoever said being in love was wonderful? Being in love was...sloppy. Confusing, sad, not at all pretty.

She whipped around, leaning one hand against the table to steady herself. "I think you'd better go now."

Josh shook his head. She couldn't possibly expect him to leave while tears were running down her cheeks. While she stood there scrubbing her eyes with her fists like a child.

But he knew her, ah, he knew her so well by now. She'd push him away the moment he tried to offer comfort, and resent any intrusion on his part because she was doing her best to build a wall between them. Even hurting as she was, she was as wild and cagey as a tigress.

But Josh knew how to handle her.

"Come on." He hooked an arm around her elbow.

She drew back. "Where?"

"Outside. For a walk."

"No."

"Just to the beach and back. Otherwise you'll wake your dad with your blubbering."

"I'm not blubbering." But she went, just as he'd hoped.

The moon had risen higher in the past half hour, and the tiny strip of beach was silvered. The tide was out and the smell of the sea was strong.

Josh seated himself in the powdery sand and pulled Rebel down beside him. She sat with her chin on her knees, her tearstained face turned away from him.

He hunted around for something to say. Strange, but he'd never had to work at words before. He finally settled on the easiest kind: smalltalk.

"I'm going to think about this place a lot when I get home. We've got weeks of winter left."

"Serves you right for living up north."

Good. Her spunk was returning, even though her voice was still thick with tears. He wished he could dry them for good by assuring her that he'd be back, but he knew better than to lie.

Let it die a quick death, Josh.

But it was hard. Harder than he'd thought.

Letting out his breath in a weary sigh, he curled his arm around her shoulder, needing her warmth, needing her. She offered no resistance, only leaned her head against him with a breathy sigh of her own.

They sat together in silence, sharing each other's pain. Two lonely people who hadn't known until they met that they were lonely at all.

Neither knew how long they sat there before

slowly, unmistakably, they both began to realize that this wasn't enough, that desire and love and pain could twine around the heart until it was impossible to tell where one ended or the other began.

Somehow, it didn't matter. Somehow, Rebel knew when to turn her face to his just as Josh lowered his head to kiss her.

She reached her arms for his neck even while he hitched her closer with his hands. The kiss was lush with familiarity, a bittersweet reunion.

She sighed her approval when he deepened the kiss, a seductive mating of tongues. His hand skimmed up her rib cage to her breast, where his thumb stroked across the sensitive nipple. Rebel's breath hitched in response and her head fell back.

"Sweet," he murmured, cupping and caressing through the filmy silk of her dress. "So sweet." His mouth moved from her lips to her jaw, trailing kisses to her collarbone while his hands continued to work their magic.

She threaded her fingers through his hair. She felt weak and weepy and breathless with desire. Josh's touch sent waves of pleasure rippling through her, everywhere.

"Rebel." His voice was rough, like his hands on her shivering skin. "I want to make love to you. I've been going crazy, pretending I don't."

She opened her eyes. Smiling, she cupped his face with her hands. "So what are you waiting for, Yankee?"

He had to laugh. Ah, Lord, there'd never been one like her. Never. His arms stayed around her as they swayed to their feet. With his mind on fire, he swept her up against him.

She laughed as he settled her against his hip and carried her toward his cottage, but the laughter turned to breathy murmurs of longing as she nuzzled his neck and trailed her lips down the line of his jaw.

Josh's heartbeat quickened. By the time he reached the bed it was fairly roaring in his ears. Shaking now, he set her down. "Wild. You make me wild," he whispered.

She kept her arms linked around his neck. Her body slid along the length of his and stayed rooted there. Up on her toes, she kept them mated, hip to hip, thigh to thigh, beating heart to heart.

He kept her there, as well, with a long, lush meeting of lips. His pulse was lurching out of control. In a vain effort to steady himself he rested his brow against hers and inhaled shakily before skimming his hands to her breasts. His palms brushed across the sensitive nipples, bringing them to straining peaks.

"Oh," Rebel said on a sigh. "Oh..."

"I've imagined this so many times."

Her eyes fluttered shut. "So have I."

Knowing that she'd dreamed of him aroused him unbearably. His stomach clenched with desire and he reached up to untie the halter straps around her neck, letting the bodice of the dress fall to her waist.

She was wearing nothing underneath. In the darkness he bent his head to her bared breasts. Showed her what it meant to be seduced by a laving, worshiping touch of mouth and tongue and teeth until her whole body trembled.

"Josh." His name was a drawn-out sigh. "Oh, Josh, I want..."

"I know what you want," he growled against her lips. His arm curved around the small of her back, bending her like a blade of grass. His lips trailed along the column of her throat while his other hand sent the wisp of a dress slithering down her legs. His fingers hooked the lace at her panties and she made a sound low in her throat. He could feel his mouth beginning to water and cautioned himself to show restraint. Slowly, slowly, he drew the panties down to pool with her dress on the floor.

Still, it was hard to wait when he burned like this, when his heart roared in his ears and Rebel quivered at his touch. So he touched her everywhere. Stroking, caressing, making her silky skin shiver. Naked, she was brown and slim, more beautiful than he'd imagined.

"Do you know how much I want you?"

She felt him straining against her and laughed. He laughed, too, roughly, then covered her mouth in a kiss that left no room for humor.

Only hunger.

As he deepened the kiss she fumbled with his shirt. Drew it off so that she could feel the bruising beat of his heart beneath her palms. He reached for the snap on his shorts but she pushed his hands away.

"Let me."

Naked at last, locked together, they sank onto the bed. Josh rose over her, elbows propped on either side of her head. Her short, dark hair made a halo against the pillow. Her eyes were black pools of longing.

Watching her intently, he showed her what it meant to receive pleasure that was almost pain. Showed her how his big hands could bend her willowy body to his bidding. Made her gasp and whisper his name and arch beneath the magic of his seeking mouth and hands. Finally, he had to close his eyes against the dazzle in hers.

"I still don't understand what you do to me, you fisherman's daughter." His voice was raw with desire.

She linked her arms around his neck. "Neither do I, you millionaire's son."

They smiled at each other, smiles that caught in the throat as the pounding of their pulses reached a single, clamoring beat. Once more he reared above her, his eyes intent on her passion-flushed face, touching her intimately with that most intimate part of himself.

"Josh," she whispered, her head falling back.

He understood. His own eyes darkened. He, too, could wait no longer.

But although he might burn, he lowered himself slowly, treasuring that special moment. Placing himself just inside her he said her name, softly. Her beautiful eyes opened. Watching her, loving her, he slipped inside to bind her, body and soul.

She gave a smothered groan of delight. Weighted with pleasure, her eyes drifted shut. Her hips arched beneath him and her hands played across his back. She would have prolonged the moment, but couldn't.

Neither could he. Desire had outstripped tenderness the moment he'd thrust himself into her moist sheath. He began moving, slowly, oh, so slowly, although everything within him cried out for release.

"Rebel, wild, sweet Rebel." He increased the pace while his heart thundered. Wild thoughts raced through his head.

Then they were gone. Need and want and a piercing pleasure had flung them aside. He turned his face into her neck, groaning, as his body shuddered and shook.

She cried out as he poured himself into her. Arched her body as her head fell back and his name burst in stunned wonder from her lips. Over the edge she was swept, in a rising tide that broke at last with shattering force upon her mind, her soul, her heart.

Chapter Ten

Afterward they lay cocooned in each other's arms, waiting for the tilting world to right itself again. Rebel had the feeling that maybe it wasn't going to, because this was what being in love with Josh was all about—this crazy whirling and wheeling, like walking along a slippery deck in stormy seas. Calm waters were definitely not in the forecast.

Not that she cared. This was the sort of weather she loved best.

But, oh, how it hurt. Because she knew that the future wasn't wild and stormy with wonder, but weighted with pain. The ache of knowing he was leaving, that tomorrow he'd be gone.

She squeezed her eyes shut against the truth. Buried her nose in the warm curve of his neck. Sighed when she felt him stir and trace kisses across her cheekbone to her temple.

"You all right, McCade?"

She smiled in the dark. "Never better."

"Good."

Rolling over onto his back he took her with him. They lay with their legs tangled, hips joined, Rebel's cheek on his chest. Keeping her eyes closed she listened to the strong, steady beat of his heart. Tomorrow night, lying all alone, she'd have nothing but the memory.

They were quiet for a long time. Josh's hand trailed lazily down her spine. Rebel felt her eyelids growing heavy. The lassitude of contentment, the pleasure of his touch, were making her sleepy.

"I wish I could stay."

She stirred. "What?"

"I wish I could stay. Here in Florida. Just a little longer."

She came up on an elbow, then traced a finger across his jaw. She was careful to keep her voice light. "Why don't you?"

"I've been away long enough."

"I thought you were the boss."

"All the more reason to get back."

"There has to be someone who—"

His arms slid from her waist to her shoulders, tightening so that he could pull her back down on top of him. "There isn't."

"What about Reardon? Why couldn't he—"

"Rebel, we've been over this before. I didn't want to talk about it then, and I don't want to now."

"Okay."

He lay there, ticking off the seconds in his head. He'd given her ten, but of course she took less than five.

"But what if I told you—"

Laughing, he flipped her over onto her back, nuzzling her, silencing her with the pressure of his mouth on hers. "Rebel, please."

She was quiet for the space of a long, indrawn breath. A gathering of courage. "I talked to Reardon on the phone today."

He lifted his head. "You what?"

"I called him up while you were in Marathon. We had a long talk, Josh." Her tone was eager. "I had no idea he worked at Alden-Moore. You never told me. And he isn't stupid, Josh. He knows what's going on. More than you think."

He didn't say a word, so she plunged on quickly. "It wouldn't be the way you said, that something awful would happen if he took over your responsibilities. That's just an excuse you've been using all these years. Besides, he has that guy...Tony? The two them together could—"

"Those were Reardon's words?"

"More or less."

"So now you've got me quitting my job, not just extending my vacation."

"Please, don't be mad." She kissed his cheek, his jaw, the cleft in his chin she loved so much. "All he wants, what I want, is what's best for you."

"Ah."

"Your mother said so, too."

"My...mother?"

"Um-hmm. She was there when I phoned. Asked if she could speak to me. We had a wonderful conversation, Josh."

"The two of you talked," he said slowly. "You and my mother."

"She was very sweet."

"She was?"

Rebel nodded against his chest.

He lay there disbelieving. Awed. He couldn't accept the fact that Helena Alden had been pleasant enough to Rebel on the phone to be termed "sweet." Then again, he shouldn't wonder that Rebel had managed to pull it off. She could charm the birds out of the trees, as the old saying went.

But Josh was far from charmed. Or pleased. The fact that Rebel had called up Reardon, discussed something with him he'd expressly forbidden her to...and then to do so with his mother, as well!

He closed his eyes, grappling with a mounting sense of frustration and betrayal. He could already picture the greeting he'd get coming home. His mother had always been convinced he worked too many hours and should delegate authority. Now to have her fires fueled by someone with a mouth like Rebel's…!

"You had no right."

Her heart stilled at his tone. "Josh, I care about you."

"That still doesn't mean you know what's best for me."

"Don't I?"

"No." He sat up, scrubbing his hands through his hair in an effort to calm himself. "You've gotten hold of this crazy idea that I'd prefer going back into medicine."

"It isn't crazy, Josh. It's what I believe. And I think you do, too, deep down."

He snorted and turned away from her.

"Josh." She came up on her knees and ran her palms over his back. So tense, so rigid, were the muscles there. She kept her voice light even though she was beginning to realize the extent of his anger. "I want you to be happy. To look back on your life when you're old and say, yeah, I did the right thing. Absolutely no regrets."

"That's ridiculous. Infantile." His tone suggested that she might be, too.

She refused to be hurt. Somebody had to make him see that he no longer owed his father a thing. Helena Alden had been so adamant in her agreement that Rebel had felt all her doubts fleeing. She'd been nervous at first, talking with Josh's mother, especially when she'd first heard that imperious, well-bred voice coming down the wire. But they'd warmed to each other quickly, both of them surprised, then pleased, by that, and Rebel had hung up with a new sense of certainty concerning Josh.

Buoyed by that certainty, she said, "Sometimes the most important things in life are so ridiculously simple that we don't always see them."

"Oh, great. You're a philosopher, too." He knew he was being hurtful, but there was no way to stem the rising tide of despair. Didn't she know that nothing was simple? Not for him, not anymore. Not now that he'd taken this wildly alluring woman to bed and discovered that she'd managed to work her way into his heart, after all, and that he had to struggle now to find some way to cast her out.

"Sorry, but we can't all give up on the real world, Rebel, and live a fantasy life like yours."

That scored a hit. She sank back on her heels and gripped her hands tightly together. "It's easy to change the system when you're simple fishing folk, is that what you're saying? That rich people live by different rules?"

"That isn't what I meant," he snapped. "I just want you to understand once and for all that you've got no right to make decisions for me. To go behind my back. To rile up my cousin and my mother with crazy misconceptions. For crying out loud, they'll never give me a moment's peace after this."

"Maybe because they're already aware of what you aren't willing to admit."

"And what is that exactly?"

"That you should be practicing medicine. That you're a born doctor, not an administrator."

Too close. She'd hit too close to his heart on that one. Even his cousin and mother had never dreamed what Rebel seemed to understand so completely—that he had buried himself in his work because it was easier than admitting he'd been doing the wrong thing with his life ever since his father's stroke.

"I'm sure you could go back to medical school for a while to brush up on your skills. You shouldn't have any problem setting up in private practice, or joining a hospital or clinic."

Josh shook his head. Her ignorance was amazing. How could she sit there and throw out advice so eagerly? Did she really think it would be that easy? It was time to put an end to such nonsense.

"Sorry, Rebel, but I've heard enough." Sliding from the bed, he began pulling on his shorts.

"Josh, wait."

"No." His voice was hard. "You seem to have this grand idea that I should resign from Alden-Moore and go back into private practice. Just like that."

"I didn't say it would be easy."

"It's impossible. Out of the question. I want you to get that through your head once and for all."

"But, Josh—"

She'd scooted to the edge of the bed and was looking up at him with those big dark eyes all eager and trusting. God, just knowing how much she believed in this made his chest ache. What would it take to sever this clutch she had around his heart?

"You don't have a clue." His voice was like a lash. "You've no idea what goes on out there in the real world. How can you?"

"Because I've been there." Rebel spoke quietly.

"Have you? Have you seen enough of life to know what's best for all of us? How'd you manage that, living here in a fish camp?"

She caught her breath, feeling the pain of his mockery slice through her heart, spilling like blood, spreading hurt everywhere. "Not here, Josh." Her voice shook. "Lots of places. I spent nearly four years working for Boynton Engineering in Des Moines."

His head came up. His hands stilled on the buttons of his shirt. "The aeronautics firm? What did you do for them?"

"Systems wiring, mainly."

"You're kidding."

She shook her head. "I was still in graduate school when they hired me. After I got my master's, they sent me all over the country."

"You have a master's? In what?"

"Electrical engineering."

He didn't know what to say. His perception of her was turned completely upside down. When Harp Jennings had mentioned to him that Rebel had gone to college, he hadn't dreamed she'd accomplished so much. There seemed to be no end to the surprises of knowing Rebel, of loving her. Peeling back the layers of her wondrous personality was a delight he wished he had the time, the luxury, to indulge in. But he didn't. He couldn't. *And he didn't love her.* For God's sake, it was just the novelty of being with her, getting to know her, making love to her...

"And now you're here." He made sure his voice was suitably cold. "You gave up a career with Boynton Engineering—"

"To run a fish camp." She lifted her chin. "That's right. You know why? Because I wasn't happy working eighty-hour weeks and spending my nights in one airport motel after another, never seeing the ocean, the palm trees. When Pop offered me the chance to come home, to crew for him, to cook for our guests, I jumped on it. It wasn't easy, but you know what? The world didn't end. Boynton Engineering didn't collapse. No disasters for them, no regrets for me."

She slipped off the bed, grateful for the darkness that hid her tears. "I may not make the money I once did, but I'm happy with what I do, Josh. And I'm not a total failure. When the season's over or we don't have any charters booked, I wire boats. Not just here, but all over the state. I've even been called down to the navy base on occasion to do some consulting for them. Does that qualify for your respect? I know cleaning house and filleting fish certainly doesn't."

He took that one on the chin, knowing he'd deserved it. But his heart clenched because of the way he'd hurt her.

"Rebel—"

She brushed past him on her way to the door, praying she wouldn't bump into anything on the way out, desperate to keep the sobs that were tearing at her throat inside before he could hear them.

He caught up with her in two swift strides. Grabbing her elbow he jerked her back. She went whirling against him, the tips of her breasts brushing his shirtfront.

"You going to run back to the house stark naked?"

At any other time she would have laughed. He was hoping she would. But she wrenched free without a word and snatched up her clothes. On her way to the door she pulled the dress down over her head, adjusted the halter straps even as she vanished outside.

The silence she left was deafening. Josh broke it by cursing savagely.

Fine. Let it end right here. What could be better? She'd calm down after he left. He'd come to his senses once he got home, and everything would be just as it had been before.

The feeling in his heart? That should fade quickly enough. Just wait and see, he told himself.

Chapter Eleven

The phone started ringing as Rebel came up the porch steps. Her heart leapt. Lee had promised to call the minute he found out whether or not he'd made the third semester honor roll. He'd been promised the entire summer in Florida by his mother if he made good grades all year.

Juggling grocery bags and keys she lifted the receiver. "McCades'."

"Would you mind telling me what you've done to Josh?"

"Excuse me?"

"I want to know what you've done to him. What you said before he left."

"Reardon?"

"Yes, it's Reardon. A miserable wretch of a Reardon who is about to go insane thanks to the endless abuse of that monster you sent home to us."

Rebel eased the groceries onto the counter. "I'm really sorry, but I'm not following you."

"Then let me spell it out. Ever since he came home, Josh has been an absolute ogre, snarling at everybody, turning his secretary into jelly, reducing the receptionists to tears. I myself have had to endure untold torture, hour after hour. You can't imagine the effect it's had on my delicate psyche."

"Not pretty, I'm sure." She hoped she sounded suitably flippant. That she was giving him the sort of response he would expect from her. Not for a minute was she about to let him know that she was still hurting. Badly.

Actually, she'd gotten pretty good at pretending she wasn't. Most people probably didn't have a clue. But this was different. This was Josh's cousin she was talking to, and they were talking about Josh.

Gripping the receiver tightly, she forced out an uncaring laugh. "Believe me, I sympathize, but what am I supposed to do? It's not my fault."

"Isn't it?"

"No."

"Whoo boy. Just like Josh. Total denial."

Now that was the sort of talk she could handle. "Yeah? Give me one good reason why I'm at fault."

"I can't believe this. I could almost be speaking to Josh, you know that? The two of you sound completely alike. Would somebody please tell me what I'm supposed to do with two such incredibly stubborn people?" Rebel could almost picture Reardon's eyes rolling toward the ceiling.

She swallowed against the sudden tightness in her throat. She didn't feel like teasing anymore. "I did what I thought best."

"I know you did, darling."

"I was wrong. We all were."

"No." Reardon was suddenly serious, too. "I'm still behind you on this one. I still believe that whatever happened to Josh on that island of yours is the best thing that's happened to him ever. But because he won't admit as much to himself, it's driving him mad, and of course he's making all of us suffer."

"That's what I said. I was wrong."

"Do you honestly believe that?"

Rebel didn't know.

"Darling, think. For years we've been watching Josh work himself into an early grave. You're the first one who's ever had the courage to call him on the floor for it. Lord knows Aunt Helena's tried, but she's not exactly what you'd call a forceful person. You are. I don't know how you figured him out so quick, but you did, and of course he resents you for it. I just wish he wouldn't drag the rest of us into it," he ended glumly.

"I'm sorry," Rebel whispered.

"Don't be. I didn't call you up to make you upset."

It was amazing how quickly she and Reardon had grown close, Rebel thought, especially when most of their interaction had happened over the phone. She knew from talking with Josh's mother weeks ago that Reardon had led something of a wild and irresponsible youth, but that those days were over. Helena, and Reardon himself, had insisted that he'd changed and Rebel believed them.

Only Josh wouldn't. Only Josh refused to come around, to dismantle the barrier he'd erected when he left Florida more than a month ago without so much as saying goodbye. Now he was making everyone miserable, and for the life of her Rebel couldn't understand why.

After all, he was finished with her. He didn't care, had never cared. He'd never said anything, not one single word, to make her believe otherwise. Why, then, had she been stupid enough to entertain the notion that what she'd found with him had amounted to more than a brief affair?

Now, no matter what Reardon said, she knew in her heart that she'd messed up everything. Misread what was in Josh's eyes, in his touch, in the way he'd made love to her that last, magical night. She could feel the hurt of that knowledge clawing at her still.

"Reb? You there?"

"Yes."

"Look, there isn't any chance that you could give Josh a call? Let him know—"

"No."

"Even if I told you—"

"Not a chance."

A heavy sigh came down the wire. "I didn't think so. But I still wanted to give it a shot. Find some way to make the big jerk open his eyes. See the two of you reconciled."

"Reconciled?" Rebel was incredulous. "You mean, as in getting back together?"

"Oh, come, darling. I was down there myself, remember? I'm not blind."

"It was a physical thing, okay? Let it go."

"Reb—"

"Please. That isn't why I called you that day." She had never dreamed even for a moment that she had a shot at landing Josh. What on earth was Reardon thinking? That Josh should throw away everything, his life in Providence, his family and friends, and come down to the Keys to become a *country doctor*? Nobody was that dumb.

"Look, I'm late for a meeting." Reardon sounded disappointed. What had he expected? "Just think about what I said, darling. Promise?"

She closed her eyes wearily. "I will."

He mumbled something that sounded like, "Sure. You and Josh both." Then he blew a noisy kiss down the wire, wished her well and hung up.

Rebel stood without moving until the telephone

began to beep, loudly and insistently. Hanging up, she spun away, her eyes bright with unshed tears. Kicking savagely at the refrigerator she slammed out of the door, fists punching the air. "Darn you to hell and back, Reardon Tate!"

At supper Pop was in a sour mood. He'd had to cancel a charter in order to get his cast off, and the thought of all that lost income was obviously not sitting well with him. He kept glaring at her while he cut his meat and chewed and swallowed, but she refused to meet his eyes. He put down his steak knife at last and growled like a bothered bear.

"Know what I think?"

"What?"

"Either you fly up to Rhode Island and tweak that Alden fellow's ear good and proper, or find yourself another boyfriend down here right quick."

Rebel laid down her own knife. It made a loud chink against the china. "Don't you start with me, Pop, or I swear I'll box *your* ears."

"Yeah? Maybe you should. Maybe you'd quit creepin' around the house like a lovesick goose if you beat up on something."

She eyed him. That balding head of his would make a tempting target.

He waved the gnawed T-bone at her. "Since when did you let somebody else start calling the shots?"

"Since when did this become your business?"

"Rebel—"

"Pop—"

They glared at each other, chins thrust in mutual anger. Then Pop sighed. "You ain't been the same since Alden left."

"That doesn't mean I'm going to call him up and beg him to come back."

"Maybe I will."

"Try it, and you'll get a cast on your other leg. I mean it, Pop. You interfere in this—"

"Okay, okay."

"You mean it?"

"I was only kidding. Jeez."

"Thank you."

Silence. But not for long.

"I just want to know why you're letting him go without a fight. It ain't like you."

Rebel's shoulders sagged. She didn't have the will to be angry anymore. "Why should I fight for him, Pop? We talked about this when you were in the hospital, remember? You think he'd settle for this—" she waved her fork at the porch ceiling "—this rundown fish camp in place of Providence?"

Pop didn't seem to take offense. "I don't know. I never been there."

"Well, neither have I. But Reardon told me the Aldens don't live in town. They're out in the country someplace, and the countryside is beautiful."

"You said Josh lived with his mother."

"Yeah, but the house is so big they've got their own wings or something like that."

"It's still time he got a place of his own."

"Not down here, Pop. Not in the Keys. If he does go back into medicine, I'm sure he'll find some prestigious clinic or private practice up north somewhere."

Pop waved the bone around some more. "So you're being totally selfless about this? Alden's welfare is all you care about?"

It's all I *have* to care about, Rebel thought sadly. He doesn't want me. He doesn't care. "That's right."

He snorted. "He's a jackass, to turn down a woman like you."

"Pop—" But she had to smile at him, even while her heart was hurting. "Thanks."

"Anytime."

She stood and started stacking the dishes. "How about dessert?"

"Maybe if you talked to him, just once, then maybe he'd… You never did say a word to him, did you?"

"About what?"

"Your feelings, darn it."

Rebel shook her head.

Pop sat back. "Well, there you have it. Both of you, keeping mum, tiptoein' around each other, never communicatin' your feelings to each other! No wonder he left!"

"This from a man with a perfect track record," Rebel muttered, not unkindly.

"You never once told him how you felt, huh?"

"It wouldn't have made any difference," Rebel said angrily.

"How do you know?"

"Because he doesn't love me." She leaned down, nose to nose with him, and said the words distinctly. "He doesn't love me. You can't expect him to give up his whole life, his home and family, for somebody he doesn't love, do you understand that? I hope so, because that's all I have to say."

She marched into the kitchen, arms full of dishes, leaving Pop glaring after her.

"Besides." Her head and one shoulder appeared around the door. "You just wish it were true so you'd end up with a wealthy son-in-law."

"Rebel!" Pop was on his feet, bellowing. "That's not fair! It ain't true! You don't think I got my own girl's best interests at heart?"

She peeked around at him again. "Nope."

He ranted a while longer, but with only half a heart. Deep down he was pleased to have her teasing him again, even if what she said was utterly, totally ridiculous. Josh Alden's money had nothing to do with Rebel's happiness. Nothing!

Although it would be a nice little bonus...

He was doing paperwork in the library when she came downstairs an hour later. An appreciative smile lit his weatherbeaten face. She looked enchanting in a creamy white dress that deepened the blue of her eyes and made her dark hair shine like jet. She was wearing sandals, and earrings that brushed her slim shoulders, and she wore about her the faint, tempting scent of perfume.

Pop's eyes narrowed all of a sudden. "Where you going?"

"Callahan's. I thought I'd take your advice. Find me a local boy and settle down."

"Rebel, you wouldn't dare."

"You never know. Don't wait up."

Her lips brushed the top of his head and then she was gone with a swish of silk, taking the scent of sunshine and flowers with her. The screen door slammed and Monster started screaming. Down at the docks the boat motor caught, then roared away.

Pop fisted his hand beneath his chin. Closed his eyes and growled low in his throat. Lord, what to do when your child was hurting?

The sensible thing, of course. Stay out of it, the way Rebel had asked.

Since when?

Shoving back from the table, he crossed to the phone, thumbed through the phone book until he found the area code he was looking for. No dice. Directory assistance said the Alden number was unlisted.

Undeterred, Pop called Harper Jennings and left a message. Then he waited in a fever of impatience until Harp rang him back. If Rebel came home early and caught him doing this…

"Don't even think about it, old man," he muttered aloud. "I'll be dead meat."

It took a while, but at long last Pop had the right number, heard the ringing at the end of the line, suffered through the interrogation of an impossibly stuffy butler-type person before he was finally connected with Josh. He'd already made out to the servant that it was an emergency, and Josh's tone was already tense when he came on the wire.

Pleased, Pop had to shove down a triumphant smile and remember to keep his voice suitably grave. To someone listening at the library door, the one-sided conversation would have sounded intensely intriguing. Good thing Rebel wasn't around to hear it.

"Glad I finally got through to you, son," Pop said gravely, leaning back comfortably in his chair. "'Cause I need help bad. It's Rebel. Yeah, bad news. Real bad, I'm afraid. She's had an accident with the boat. A run-in with a piling."

He winced at the thought because it sort of pricked his pride. He'd taught the girl to handle boats almost straight out of toddlerhood. Still, it was all he'd been able to think of on the spur of the moment.

"Hurt? Yeah, I'm startin' to think so. Trouble is, she refuses to go see the doctor. I been talking myself blue in the face but she keeps tellin' me…

What? Oh, earlier today. She's been in bed ever since. Says she has a headache. Doesn't do anything but sleep. When she was awake just now she was seeing double, which doesn't surprise me considering that bump on her forehead. A real goose egg. But she drifted off again after supper. Can't hardly wake her to save my life.''

He was proud of himself. He'd thrown in enough symptoms to make Josh suspect a serious problem. And all of them were real. He'd learned them just the other night, on an old rerun of "Matlock."

"What's that?" Now Pop leaned forward in his chair. "Heck, no, there's no need for you to come all the way down here! I just need some advice on how to get her stubborn little butt over to the clinic. I thought maybe you'd have a suggestion considerin' the two of you got on so well and she thinks the world— Yeah? Okay, if you insist. Couldn't hurt, I guess." Pop reached for a pad and pencil, being very, very careful to keep on sounding like a desperate father at the end of his tether.

"The next flight, huh? Just let me know the number and when it's due and I'll pick you up. What's that? Yeah, it *is* an old car, but you don't have to go and rent... Okay, a new one'd be a whole lot more dependable, I agree. Right. So I guess I'll see you when—" He broke off because the line had gone dead. Usually he lost his temper whenever anybody dared hang up on him, but this time he merely leaned back in his chair, laced his hands over his stomach and allowed himself a grin of smug satisfaction.

It was going on two o'clock in the morning when Rebel eased the boat up against the McCades' dock. Even though she'd realized that Callahan's was a mistake from the moment she'd stepped through the door, she'd made herself stay. Memories of the evening she'd spent there with Josh were like fresh wounds in her heart, and she'd had no choice but to forge new memories, to rub him out as though he'd never been, by dancing with other men, sharing laughter with friends, drinking a daiquiri for old times' sake.

She'd hated every minute of it.

But at least she was tired now. Exhausted, really. The past six weeks had been fully booked with charters and she and Pop had worked hard every minute. But maybe she'd sleep well tonight. Lord knows she hadn't been lately.

"Reb? That you?"

It was Pop, hobbling down the path with a flashlight. She was deeply touched. He hadn't waited up for her in years. She jumped down beside him. "Hi."

He put his arm around her shoulders and gave her a quick squeeze. "Have a good time?"

"Lousy."

"Aww. That's too bad."

She gave him a sharp glance. He didn't sound

very sorry. "Mind if I sleep in tomorrow? I'm really tired."

"Whatever you like."

"We were going to pull that engine, remember?"

"No problem. We'll start after lunch. 'Night, sweetie."

She started up the path, then turned to squint at him through the darkness. "You okay, Pop?"

"Fine, just fine."

"Good." But she continued to stare at him suspiciously. He was acting the way he always did whenever he had some kind of despicable plan up his sleeve. All cagey, shifty-eyed and eager, like a weasel in a henhouse.

Sure enough, she'd barely turned away again when the running lights of a boat hove into view around the tiny spit of land that separated their dockage from the bay.

"Pop, somebody's coming."

He flicked the flashlight upward and caught the white of a hull. "Hey, you're right."

"What's going on? Why would somebody come out to see us at this hour?"

He glanced at her, but said nothing. A searchlight came on and Pop stumped down to the end of the dock to guide the boat in. Rebel followed, her heart beating with the certainty that something terrible had happened.

Even before the boat had drawn alongside, a tall

shape waiting in the bow jumped across the distance to the dock. "Pop! Where's Rebel?"

Dear God, it was Josh.

"Right over there."

Josh whirled, looking stunned. "Rebel! What in hell—? What are you doing out of bed?"

Pop looked quickly toward the shadowy figure at the helm. "Who's that brought you over? Talbot? Wanna come up to the house for a beer?"

"Thanks, but I'm off." George Talbot, who ran a charter out of Marathon, was already pushing off from the dock. "Nice meeting you, Josh. See you around, Pop."

Josh didn't even notice. Catching Rebel by the shoulders he shouted above the throbbing engines, "Why in hell aren't you resting?"

She was still looking at him as though dumbstruck, aware that he was shouting at her and that he wasn't making the least bit of sense. But it didn't matter. Her heart was so full of joy that she thought it might burst.

"Rebel! Will you answer me?"

The urgency in his tone got through at last. She blinked. "Josh, why are you here?"

"To take you to the hospital, of course!"

"The hospital! Whatever for?"

"If your father couldn't convince you to see a doctor—"

"Ahem." Pop cleared his throat. "I'll leave the two of you to hash this out."

"Hold on a minute." Rebel had whirled and caught him by the back of the shirt.

"Let go the shirt, Reb."

"I smell a rat."

"Izzat so?" He was fidgeting now.

Lucky for Pop, Josh had sized up the situation fast enough and now he straightened and let go of Rebel's shoulders. But he didn't sound any less kindly than Rebel. "It was a lie?" he asked slowly, glaring at Pop.

"Not a lie," Pop said hastily. "A teeny tale I sort of made up."

Rebel swung on Josh. Her fury lashed out to encompass him, too. "What's going on? Did he call you? Is that why you're here?"

"Damned right he called me!" Josh's tone suggested that he couldn't believe even Pop capable of such colossal deceit. "He told me you'd had an accident with the boat, that you'd hit some sort of piling. The symptoms he described on the phone suggested nothing short of a closed-head injury!"

"Pop!" Rebel shrieked, turning on him. "Pop, how could you!"

"Now just a minute, Reb—" Pop was backing away as he spoke, palms upturned to ward her off. "You were so miserable that I had to do something!"

"A jump off the Seven Mile Bridge would have been good enough, Pop. It would have saved me the trouble of killing you now." Rebel was advancing on him as she spoke. Her eyes spit blue fire. Her hands were clenched into fists and she was coming at him like a boxer in a ring.

It was something to see, all right. And even though Josh was grappling with his own rage, he couldn't help but see the humor in it—the wonder of Rebel at full-throttle, stalking her old man, looking so fiery and beautiful that he wanted to sweep her into his arms.

Oh, and the relief of knowing she was okay. Of knowing that the fear that had whipped him onto that chartered plane in Providence hadn't been justified at all. In fact, it was fading rapidly now, leaving him sapped of strength. He had the sudden urge to sit down, before his legs gave out on him completely.

"Rebel." Hooking a hand around her elbow, he tugged her gently but firmly backward. "Don't hurt him. Remember, he just broke his leg."

"I'll break it again. The other one, too."

Josh's lips twitched. "There's still time for that. I may end up helping you. Right now we have to talk."

"Great. I'll make coffee," Pop said.

"Alone, Pop. I'd like to speak to Rebel alone."

"Fine, fine," the old man grumped.

"Is my old cottage empty?"

"For you, sure."

"But—"

Rebel wasn't given the chance to say anything else. Still holding her firmly by the elbow, Josh dragged her down the path toward the mint-colored cottage.

Chapter Twelve

He looked fabulous. The thought struck Rebel the moment he leaned over to turn on the lamp. A white oxford shirt and tie, a dark blue sweater knotted around his shoulders, his dark curls tousled, a bit too long, as though he'd been neglecting a badly needed haircut.

She thrust away the twinge of longing that fled through her as she studied his beloved face, and said the first thing that came to mind. "How come you're wearing a sweater?"

He grimaced. "Not a good thing down here, I agree, but I drove to the airport without bothering to change. Or to pack."

"You didn't pack?"

"I was in a hurry."

"Because you thought I'd had an accident."

He nodded. Now that they were indoors in the light she saw the strain in his eyes, the lines of fatigue around his mouth. Her heart lurched.

"Josh, I'm sorry. I don't know what my dad was thinking. He's lost his mind."

"Undoubtedly. But we'll wait a while before we kill him. Let's make him sweat a little first."

She stared at him in wonder. "Y-you're not mad."

"Not anymore."

"But—"

"Rebel, do we really have to talk about this?"

"Y-you said you wanted to."

"That was before. I'd rather be doing something else right now."

She tipped up her face as he came to stand in front of her, which was good because that way her mouth was already slanted upward so that he had no trouble lowering his head and taking it with his own.

She gasped, then sighed, then settled into him. His arm went around her, bending her back like a flower.

"Man, this is truly coming home."

"I'm so glad. Oh, Josh, when I saw you there on the dock—"

"Shh. Don't talk. Talking's for later."

And he proved as much by scooping her into his

arms and carrying her the few feet to the bed. She stayed cleaved to him as he laid her down so that he came along with her, the kiss unbroken. Slow and soft-focused, as though they had all the time in the world.

There was so much to feel, with all her senses. The rasp of Josh's wool sweater against her cheek, the thickness of his hair beneath her fingers. The scent of his after-shave and his own, familiar masculine smell. The weight of him leaning into her, the achingly gentle touch of his mouth.

At first she was content to savor this much. He was here, holding her, and her heart reveled. Sensations that she had only yearned for during the past few lonely weeks were suddenly real, filling her with a dreamy sort of wonder that had her believing in miracles.

But Josh was no dream. And as the reality of his presence sank in, slowly, deliciously, so did the stirrings of desire. A slow fire began to burn, spreading flames through pore and vein. Heat built, fanning inward toward that intimate place where they were pressed together. Rebel had committed him so much to memory that she didn't have to shift or stir as he deepened the kiss, only open herself so that they fitted together, their bodies meshed, straining against unwanted clothing.

How often had he dreamed of peeling her out of a dress? Josh wondered. Guided by memory he did so now, his hands very sure even though he was shaking inside. Fingers of fire were burning through his blood. He let them spread, everywhere, while he plundered that ripe, beautiful mouth.

"Do you know how much I've dreamed of this?"

"As much as I have." Her words ended on a sigh as he splayed his hand over her ribs and stroked his thumb across her naked breast.

"It's all I could think of back home."

"Reardon told me you were acting like a monster."

"Only because I couldn't stop thinking of you. Of this."

She gasped as he lowered his head and his tongue encircled a pink, thrusting peak.

"And this."

He worshiped the other breast with lips and tongue and teeth. Skimming his hands to her hips, he rose above her to unknot the sweater and pull off his shirt. Naked to the waist he leaned over her again, letting her feel the rasp of his skin against hers while he sought succor from her willing mouth.

"I was miserable," he whispered, admitting it at last.

"So was I."

He pressed his cheek against her hair and held her, wishing he had the means to soothe away all her hurt. "I was in a fog. I couldn't function. I probably gave millions to the undeserving."

.

"No, you didn't," she said with a tender laugh. "Reardon wouldn't have let you. Besides—" her lips brushed his temple "—I thought we weren't going to talk."

His heart turned over. She always knew what to say. How to calm his worries, make light of his troubles, let him see that being here, with her, was all that mattered.

And, Lord, how he wanted her. His body was fairly humming with need. Any moment now he was going to start shaking. He tried to swallow away the tightness in his throat while he lifted an unsteady hand to brush the hair from her brow.

Smiling, she reached for the button on his khakis but he laced her fingers through his and lifted them away. "Let me. I want to love you."

And he did. With a gentleness that left her breathless. A tenderness that drove away the hurt and the pain of those past, lonely weeks. And a passion that made her gasp and arch beneath his seeking hands. He molded her body, stroking, tasting, savoring, content to pleasure her while he came to know her all over again.

When her breath was coming in fast little pants and her skin was flushed, he rose up to capture her lips in a searing kiss. Murmuring words of endearment, he slipped his hand between her thighs to find her center, stroking and caressing with a masterful touch. She cried out and bucked beneath him.

His lips trailed across her cheek as he drove her

on, drunk with the power of knowing in that moment that she was his alone. He pleasured her slowly even though everything within him cried out for possession. His body clamored, but he continued with his relentless assault.

"Ohh," Rebel groaned as her climax shattered like glass into a thousand rainbow colors in her mind. Clinging to him she arched wildly, sobbing his name. "I love you," she gasped through clenched teeth. "Oh, Josh..."

I love you, his heart seemed to thunder in response. I love you.

Staggered by the truth, needing to join with her, he shifted and slipped inside her.

Her eyes opened wide. Her arms tightened about his shoulders as she drew him deep. Her muscles, still convulsed, closed around him. Her breath beat against his ear as they moved together in slow, wondrous rhythm.

The scent of her, the heat and softness, the faint rasping of dewed skin against skin, had Josh's mind skittering out of control. He would have preferred to prolong the moment, holding himself back while he drove her up to the edge again, but there was no time—or need. Already that sweet rippling sensation was building to overtake her and she clung to him, her head falling back.

A gathering, a moment of exquisite pain, then he turned his face into her neck as passion exploded, out of control. Cleaved to her, he called out her name, felt himself burning up in her fires as he emptied himself within her.

In a way it was painful, the sweet aftermath. The pain of knowing that this, like everything else in their relationship, was temporary at best. But Rebel wasn't going to think about it. There would be time later, after he was gone. Lots of time for thinking, remembering, grieving. She knew that now.

Thrusting away any thought of heartache, she nestled against him. He lay propped on the pillows, one arm curled around her, lazily stroking his hand down her hip.

I have him now, she thought contentedly. That's more than I ever hoped for.

It had to be enough.

Another thought occurred to her and she smiled.

His hand never stilled its gentle stroking. "What?"

"Pop. Handing you that line of bull."

"It was something, all right."

"You shouldn't have believed him."

"I had no reason not to."

She nodded, embarrassed. "He had no right to do that to you. I'm so sorry, Josh. I don't know how to make it up to you."

His hand cupped her breast. He smiled. "This is a pretty good start."

Sighing, she closed her eyes and rubbed her cheek against his chest. She felt sleepy and content.

After a minute Josh said thoughtfully, "Maybe we should go up to the house, tell him everything's okay."

"Nah. Let's make him sweat. He deserves it." Besides, she didn't want to leave the warmth of their bed. Not now, not ever. "Josh?"

"Hmm?" His voice told her he was feeling sleepy himself.

"Everything's not okay, is it?"

He opened his eyes. His voice changed. "What do you mean?"

"You came all the way from Rhode Island, took time off from work, spent a fortune on airfare, because my father lied to you. That's not okay."

"Then let's talk about it."

"Please."

"Why do you think he lied?"

Because Rebel was lying with her head on his chest, he could feel her cheek heating as she flushed with embarrassment. "Um, I really don't know."

"Now who's the liar?" His voice was amused, but only to hide his nervousness. So very much rested on her answer. "He mentioned you were miserable. Because of me?"

When she nodded, he tightened his arm around her and rested his chin on the top of her head and closed his eyes. "So was I. I was so sure everything would be better when I left. Once I got home, I knew I'd find the proper perspective for this place, for you."

Had he? She held herself very still. If so, she'd be lost. Without him there was nothing. She'd truly wanted him to be happy, to find his proper place in life, the way she had. She'd never dared to dream of anything more—certainly not for the two of them. But now she knew that her place was here, with him. She was the one who'd be cast adrift when he left.

But he'd been miserable in Rhode Island. Reardon had said so, and Josh had admitted it, too.

"The longer I stayed away, the worse it got."

"What did?" she asked, scarcely daring to breathe.

He chuckled. "Ever have an itch you couldn't scratch? Somewhere just out of reach?"

She blinked, bewildered. "I guess."

"Then you can understand what it was like for me back home. The longer I stayed, the worse it got. Until your father called. Until I stepped off George Talbot's boat and saw you."

"I stopped the itch?" Her voice was filled with confusion.

Beneath her cheek she could feel the laughter rumbling in his chest. "Completely."

"So that's why you came back? Because you needed a good scratching?"

He kept on laughing, cupping her breast again and rubbing his foot along the length of her silky leg. "Believe me, I got it."

She considered a moment. "Maybe it was just relief."

"Huh?"

"Relief. That I wasn't really in an accident."

"Now you're being practical. That's not at all like you."

"So tell me the truth, then."

"I just did."

"No. In real words. Not about having an itch nobody but me could scratch."

He hitched her closer so that she lay half across his hip. "Trust a woman to pick every little thing apart. Never to be satisfied with one explanation. Okay. Here it is. Why do you think I left Gasparilla Key without saying goodbye?"

She felt a twinge of remembered hurt. "Because you were furious with me."

"Bingo. And why was I furious? Because you'd had the nerve to accuse me outright of something I'd been denying to myself for years. You were the only one who ever understood that part of me, Rebel."

"The part that wasn't satisfied being CEO."

"Right."

"Josh, that isn't in real words."

"Wait now, I'm getting to that part. I want you to know the reason I was angry. Because I had to hear all that stuff from you, the one woman on earth who's ever seen through me, the only one I'd ever been in danger of falling in love with."

She caught her lower lip between her teeth. "Come on. You've never been in love before?"

"Not like this."

"Oh." She went still. "Ohh…"

"Yeah, it surprised me, too. That's why I had to get out of here. I was hoping your tropical sunshine was responsible for screwing up my wiring, messing with my sanity. But it was the same in Providence. Worse. No matter how hard I tried, it wouldn't go away. I'm not talking about going back into medicine, either, even though you'd been pounding that into me ever since your father broke his leg. No, it was something a hell of a lot worse."

"Worse?"

His lips twitched. "I had to come to terms with the fact that I'd fallen in love with you, anyway. You, the fisherman's daughter. A prickly, tiresome sort of woman who isn't going to give me a moment's peace for the rest of my life. A woman I just can't seem to get out of my heart." His voice dropped to a whisper. "As if I'd ever want to."

She rolled up onto one elbow, looked down at him with her own heart in her eyes. "Took you long enough to get to that part, Providence. So that's why you came back?"

"I knew I'd been denying the truth to myself the minute Pop called me. When I thought you'd been hurt—" He broke off and his mouth thinned. For a second everything he'd felt was revealed in his eyes.

No outright declaration of love could have shaken Rebel more, healed her more. Overwhelmed, she turned her head away, feeling tears thicken her throat.

"You'd given me so many demons to wrestle with, sweetheart. It just took a little while to deal with them all."

Because she still had her face averted, he added forcibly, "Not your background. Never that. That was just my very lame way of trying to beat back the feelings you kept arousing in me. I want you to know once and for all that I'm honored and proud to have your love. Rebel McCade, you humble me."

When she turned toward him, he saw the tears glistening on her lashes in the soft glow from the lamp in the other room. His heart stilled. "You're crying."

She rubbed the heel of her hand across her face. "I know."

"You hate crying."

"Not this time."

His heart suddenly seemed too big for his chest. Drawing her down on top of him, he laced his fingers through hers, then laid their joined hands upon his heart so that she could feel its wild, heady beat. "That was beautiful," he managed, "but this time I want to hear the real words, too."

"I love you, Josh."

His fingers tightened around hers. "Say it again."

"I love you." Bending her head, her mouth found his. "I love you, you impossibly stubborn millionaire's son. Lee told me you were thick, and you know what? He was right."

"I could have saved us a lot of heartache if I'd given in right away," he agreed, unoffended.

"Think of the airfare you could've saved."

They smiled at each other. Offered their mouths in a kiss that was glorious with emotion. Tongues mated, lips tasted, breath gusted gently.

"I'm going to marry you, you know." Josh lifted his mouth from hers as he said this, and it gave her the moment she needed to recover from the shock.

"I know."

"Sure you do."

"I mean it."

"Liar."

She grinned, her impish Rebel's grin. "Care to arm wrestle over that, Providence?"

"Too late." Rolling fully on top of her, he captured her arms on either side of her head. "I've won, and you are now my prisoner. You'll never escape."

As if she ever wanted to. There were stars in her eyes when she looked at him. "I suppose that means you can do with me as you will."

His own eyes gleamed. "Believe me, I intend to."

* * *

The sun was barely showing through the blinds when Rebel stirred, then lifted her head from the pillow beside him. Yawning, rubbing her eyes, she grinned suddenly and rolled over to straddle him.

"Josh."

No answer.

"Josh."

"Hmm."

"You said last night you'd marry me. I haven't heard a proposal."

He groaned. "What time is it?"

"Six."

"Rebel, we've had less than three hours' sleep."

She bent her head until her mouth hovered just above his. "I want that proposal, Josh."

"It's on my desk," he mumbled.

Smiling, she rubbed her palms over his shoulders while her lips nipped ever so gently at his. "Wake up, you goof. You're not in your office."

He stirred reluctantly, then opened his eyes. Rebel's smile deepened because his gaze was so unfocused. And because he looked so cute with his hair tousled and that manly shadow darkening his unshaven jaw. "Would you like some coffee first?" she asked.

"Before what?"

"You propose to me."

"Man. Oh, man. I'll need way more to fortify myself enough for that."

"Oh? Like what?"

"Breakfast. Lunch. Supper. A couple of days in the gym. A week of—"

She silenced him by tracing the shape of his mouth with her tongue. Nipping and tasting, she held him by the wrists with his arms on either side of his head, the way he'd captured her the night before.

"You're playing with fire," he managed, glad that he could speak at all.

"You can't scare me, Josh Alden. I'm a big girl."

"Prove it."

And she did.

Two hours later, showered, shaved and ravenously hungry, Josh insisted that they make an appearance at the house for breakfast. Hand in hand they strolled up the path, their arrival on the terrace announced by a joyously barking Yellow Dog.

Pop appeared at the porch door, Monster on his arm. His face was shadowed by a baseball cap, impossible to read.

Josh leaned down to whisper in Rebel's ear. "Does he look mad?"

"Why should he be mad?"

"Considering I kept you with me all night..."

"I think he looks more nervous than mad."

"Hopefully. But we still have some explaining to do."

Rebel tossed her head. "So does he."

Pop stepped aside to let them in. "Mornin'."

There, that proved he was nervous. Saying good-morning was the way Pop thought people should act when they were being genial. And he was never genial unless he was feeling guilty about something. Rebel let go of Josh's hand and made sure she was scowling when she swung around to face him.

"Pop—"

He held up his hand, gesturing behind him. "Wait, don't say a word. Eat first."

Rebel turned and felt her jaw drop. He'd set the porch table with the better china, the kind reserved for guests. Flowers crammed into an empty beer bottle served as a centerpiece. Slices of toast, slightly burned, lay in the basket along with bacon that had seen the bottom of a pan too long. There were scrambled eggs with pieces of shell in them and grits that had the consistency of wallboard paste.

"Pop, you made breakfast. It looks…delicious."

"Least I could do."

Josh stepped over to the sideboard to pour a cup of coffee. Rebel saw him gag as he took a sip.

Pop regarded him anxiously. "Too strong?"

"No, it's fine. I like my coffee solid, uh, strong."

"Oh, that. I might've spilled a few grounds in the pot."

"It's fine. Really."

Pop pulled out a chair. "Come on, Reb. Have a seat."

She shook her head, finally deciding to take pity on him. "It's okay, Pop, you can drop the act. We're not mad anymore."

"Is that what this is all about?" Josh asked, startled.

"Well, I was sort of hopin' to butter you up."

"And here I was thinking you'd be pounding on my door demanding a shotgun wedding."

Pop's eyes glinted. "If I thought for a minute you weren't going to marry my little girl—"

"You'd be up here bawling your eyes out," Rebel said with a grin, "feeling sorry for yourself, not me, because Josh's money was flying out the door before you ever had the chance to get your hands on it."

Pop turned scarlet. It was the first time in her life Rebel had seen him blush. "Now, Reb. That ain't at all true." He cast a despairing glance at Josh. "See what I gotta put up with?"

Rebel's grin faded. She turned serious. "It's okay, Pop. I understand."

This breakfast, no matter how inedible, was Pop's way of showing his love. So was the way he'd interfered yesterday, although she'd have to remember to lecture him severely about doing anything so dramatic in the future.

But right now they had something else to tell him, something far more important. Turning her head, she looked at Josh. He was already setting down his coffee cup and coming to stand behind her.

Putting his hands on her shoulders, he said earnestly, "Now that you mention money, I want you to know that times are going to be a little tough for a while."

Pop scowled. "How do you mean?"

"Only that it's going to take some time to get my career up and running. I'll have to brush up on my skills first, get licensed to practice medicine in the state of Florida, then convince the locals they've got themselves a fine new doctor."

Rebel took one of his hands in hers and brought it to her cheek. "That'll be the easy part."

Pop's eyes were nearly bugging out of his head. "You mean you're gonna stay here? Do your doctorin' in the Keys?"

"I couldn't ask Rebel to give up crewing for you, could I? Not when I've already demanded plenty this morning by asking her to be my wife."

"That's going to be hard enough," Rebel agreed, her eyes shining.

They both looked back at Pop. He was fumbling in his shirt pocket for a cigar. Clamping it between his teeth, he collapsed heavily on a nearby chair. Brow furrowed, he sat there chewing and thinking.

"We'll have to live here for a while, too," Josh went on, exchanging glances with Rebel. "Later we'll probably move to Crawl or Grassy Key."

"Marathon's too crowded," Rebel agreed.

"Rebel doesn't mind commuting to work by boat," Josh went on, "but I'll be on call a lot, so I can't afford to be too far from my patients."

"Or the emergency room. We've given this a lot of thought, Pop. Talked it through. What do you think?"

Pop said nothing. Just sat there and chewed.

Rebel's hand sought Josh's. His fingers closed around hers, squeezing reassuringly.

At last Pop cut his eyes at Josh. "You in love with her?"

"Yes."

"Gonna make her happy?"

"He already has, Pop."

Pop snorted. Anybody with eyes in his head could see that. The way she looked at him, and he at her. The way they held hands, stood so close together.

He got up with a growl. "Then I guess I got no objections."

"That's great, Pop." Josh shook the offered hand and kept his arm around Rebel while Pop kissed the top of her head.

"How about breakfast?" she asked, her voice a little unsteady because she was so swamped with emotion. "Will you join us, Pop?"

"Can't right now. I'm busy."

"Doing what? Hey! Where are you going?"

Pop swung around in the doorway. "Gotta call the printer's. Change our brochures."

"Now? What for?"

"We gotta raise our rates."

"Pop! Why?"

"Well, why not?" He grinned at them, his chest puffing with pride. "We got ourselves the best charter business in the Keys now that we got us our own doctor in the house!"

Epilogue

On his way down the corridor, Josh paused to stick his head in the waiting room. Empty. He leaned back with a sigh of relief.

Nellie, his receptionist, smiled at him from the other side of her desk. "Busy morning."

"I'll say. Who's next?"

She glanced at the computer screen. "One more in Room 3, then a break for lunch."

"Sure can use it." Josh ran his hands through his hair. "Any calls from my wife?"

"Not yet."

He frowned. Even though Rebel was only six months' pregnant, he insisted that she call him regularly at the clinic. Not for medical reasons, of course, but for his own peace of mind. In his opinion she was working too hard, taking on too much, especially now that she'd started painting and redecorating the cottage they'd recently bought.

At least he'd taken the precaution of forbidding her to go out in the boat with Pop once her pregnancy was confirmed. Naturally the decision hadn't gone over too well with Rebel, who was always accusing him of worrying too much. Insisting that as a doctor he should know better than to overcoddle a healthy mother-to-be.

"Honestly, I don't know which one of you is worse, you or Pop," she had taken to complaining, and all at once Josh could picture her face clearly in front of him, blue eyes dancing, her soft mouth curled in a sexy smile as she wagged a chiding finger under his nose.

He rubbed his chest at the thought. His heart always seemed too big to fit whenever he thought of Rebel, especially nowadays when she looked so radiant, seemed so happy. Their only regret in this first year of married life, in fact, was the hours he put in at the clinic. Neither of them had dreamed he'd end up with such a busy practice, that even before their first anniversary rolled around he'd have to add a new wing to the building just to make room for his patients.

At least Josh had made arrangements to take on a partner; by the time the baby was born he'd be able to spend plenty of time at home.

With Rebel. With their child.

The thought made him want to burst out singing.

He was hoping for a girl as beautiful and feisty as her mother.

Rebel wanted a boy.

"Why?" he'd asked her the first time she told him that.

"Because Pop'd die if I didn't provide him with a replacement when I retire."

"And what's wrong with maintaining the tradition of female crews on his charters?"

"Josh! No daughter of mine is going to spend her days crewing for that selfish, foulmouthed—"

He'd taken her face in his hands and smiled into her sparkling eyes. "You did, and look how well you turned out."

"Oh. Well, that's because...because I was lucky."

No, he was the lucky one, Josh thought. Standing in the silent corridor he massaged his breastbone again. Lord, how he missed her whenever he was away for long! It'd been hours since he'd kissed her goodbye after breakfast and left for the clinic; it would be hours more until he was done for the day.

"Dr. Alden? You okay?"

He grinned sheepishly at his receptionist. "Sorry. What were you saying about the patient in number three?"

"Nothing. We weren't discussing her at all."

Nellie did her best to sound disapproving even though everyone on staff had taken to indulging Dr. Alden for these occasional father-to-be lapses. After all, they, too, were eager for the arrival of Rebel's baby. A surprise baby shower had already been planned. Suitable names for both a girl and a boy were being discussed around the water cooler. Nellie had already bought skeins of ribbon to decorate the office when the big day arrived, pink and blue, just in case.

"Nellie?" Josh was scowling at the empty folder bracket on the back of the examining-room door. "Where's her records?"

"New patient. She insisted on being seen before lunch. I didn't think you'd mind if I slipped her in without finishing it."

Actually, he did. And it wasn't at all like Nellie. She was usually so tidy and efficient that he often wondered how he'd ever get along without her. The fact that she was kind and motherly, had raised four children of her own and had taken Rebel under her wing in all matters female had only made Josh admire her more. He was fond of her, too, as was Rebel—and Pop, though he'd probably scuttle every last one of his boats before admitting as much. But the fact remained that Josh didn't like meeting patients without reviewing their medical histories.

"Nellie, I don't even know the woman's name."

Her plump, cheery face reddened. "Oops. Neither do I. Hold on and I'll check with Susan."

But Josh's nurse had asked for an early lunch and he'd already let her go. Sighing, he knocked on the door, then let himself in. And gave a start of surprise when the woman sitting in the chair before him rose and slipped her arms around his neck.

"I thought you'd forgotten all about me, doc."

Her soft, fragrant cheek pressed against his. A gently rounded belly bumped his hip.

Josh caught her by the wrists. "Rebel! What— there isn't anything wrong, is there?"

Her laughing mouth grazed his. "No. Why?"

"You're here, checked in as a patient—"

"That was Nellie's idea. I was complaining about how busy you were, so she went ahead and scheduled me for an appointment. A long one."

"I see." Josh's lips curved into a wolfish smile. "Well, then, we'd better take a look at you. Why don't you get up on the table? Tell me what the problem is? Oh, better remove all your clothes first."

"Actually, the problem isn't with me, doctor. It's my bedroom back home."

He stared at her. "What?"

She batted her eyes innocently, looking good enough to eat. "You see, I just finished painting it, and now I'm worried about the shade."

"The shade?" he echoed stupidly. He couldn't seem to concentrate on what she was saying. It was all he could do not to unbutton the back of her dress and remove it right here and now. His hand played with the silky hair at the nape of her neck. She pressed against him like a sleek, sexy cat.

"I think it may have turned out too yellow."

Understanding dawned. His wolfish grin became even more predatory. "Ah. So you want me to take a look. Give you my professional opinion."

"That's right. Considering my appointment and the fact that you have an hour off for lunch, you should have enough time, right?"

He hitched her closer, his eyes glowing with a lusty light of their own. "I'm not sure. Convince me."

Grinning, Rebel came up on her toes and offered him her mouth.

"Hmm." A drawn-out sigh of easy pleasure escaped his lips as the kiss deepened. "Maybe I should check out that paint."

Even though he knew perfectly well that he'd be much too busy to do any looking.

*   *   *   *   *

This summer, the legend
continues in Jacobsville

Diana Palmer

A LONG, TALL
TEXAN SUMMER

Three **BRAND-NEW** short stories

This summer, Silhouette brings readers a special
collection for Diana Palmer's LONG, TALL TEXANS
fans. Diana has rounded up three **BRAND-NEW**
stories of love Texas-style, all set in Jacobsville,
Texas. Featuring the men you've grown to love from
this wonderful town, this collection is a must-have
for all fans!

*They grow 'em tall in the saddle in Texas—and
they've got love and marriage on their minds!*

Don't miss this collection of original Long, Tall Texans
stories...available in June at your favorite retail outlet.

Silhouette®

Look us up on-line at: http://www.romance.net   LTTST

MILLION DOLLAR SWEEPSTAKES
OFFICIAL RULES
NO PURCHASE NECESSARY TO ENTER

1. To enter, follow the directions published. Method of entry may vary. For eligibility, entries must be received no later than March 31, 1998. No liability is assumed for printing errors, lost, late, non-delivered or misdirected entries.

    To determine winners, the sweepstakes numbers assigned to submitted entries will be compared against a list of randomly, preselected prize winning numbers. In the event all prizes are not claimed via the return of prize winning numbers, random drawings will be held from among all other entries received to award unclaimed prizes.

2. Prize winners will be determined no later than June 30, 1998. Selection of winning numbers and random drawings are under the supervision of D. L. Blair, Inc., an independent judging organization whose decisions are final. Limit: one prize to a family or organization. No substitution will be made for any prize, except as offered. Taxes and duties on all prizes are the sole responsibility of winners. Winners will be notified by mail. Odds of winning are determined by the number of eligible entries distributed and received.

3. Sweepstakes open to residents of the U.S. (except Puerto Rico), Canada and Europe who are 18 years of age or older, except employees and immediate family members of Torstar Corp., D. L. Blair, Inc., their affiliates, subsidiaries, and all other agencies, entities, and persons connected with the use, marketing or conduct of this sweepstakes. All applicable laws and regulations apply. Sweepstakes offer void wherever prohibited by law. Any litigation within the province of Quebec respecting the conduct and awarding of a prize in this sweepstakes must be submitted to the Régie des alcools, des courses et des jeux. In order to win a prize, residents of Canada will be required to correctly answer a time-limited arithmetical skill-testing question to be administered by mail.

4. Winners of major prizes (Grand through Fourth) will be obligated to sign and return an Affidavit of Eligibility and Release of Liability within 30 days of notification. In the event of non-compliance within this time period or if a prize is returned as undeliverable, D. L. Blair, Inc. may at its sole discretion, award that prize to an alternate winner. By acceptance of their prize, winners consent to use of their names, photographs or other likeness for purposes of advertising, trade and promotion on behalf of Torstar Corp., its affiliates and subsidiaries, without further compensation unless prohibited by law. Torstar Corp. and D. L. Blair, Inc., their affiliates and subsidiaries are not responsible for errors in printing of sweepstakes and prize winning numbers. In the event a duplication of a prize winning number occurs, a random drawing will be held from among all entries received with that prize winning number to award that prize.

5. This sweepstakes is presented by Torstar Corp., its subsidiaries and affiliates in conjunction with book, merchandise and/or product offerings. The number of prizes to be awarded and their value are as follows: Grand Prize — $1,000,000 (payable at $33,333.33 a year for 30 years); First Prize — $50,000; Second Prize — $10,000; Third Prize — $5,000; 3 Fourth Prizes — $1,000 each; 10 Fifth Prizes — $250 each; 1,000 Sixth Prizes — $10 each. Values of all prizes are in U.S. currency. Prizes in each level will be presented in different creative executions, including various currencies, vehicles, merchandise and travel. Any presentation of a prize level in a currency other than U.S. currency represents an approximate equivalent to the U.S. currency prize for that level, at that time. Prize winners will have the opportunity of selecting any prize offered for that level; however, the actual non U.S. currency equivalent prize if offered and selected, shall be awarded at the exchange rate existing at 3:00 P.M. New York time on March 31, 1998. A travel prize option, if offered and selected by winner, must be completed within 12 months of selection and is subject to: traveling companion(s) completing and returning of a Release of Liability prior to travel; and hotel and flight accommodations availability. For a current list of all prize options offered within prize levels, send a self-addressed, stamped envelope (WA residents need not affix postage) to: MILLION DOLLAR SWEEPSTAKES Prize Options, P.O. Box 4456, Blair, NE 68009-4456, USA.

6. For a list of prize winners (available after July 31, 1998) send a separate, stamped, self-addressed envelope to: MILLION DOLLAR SWEEPSTAKES Winners, P.O. Box 4459, Blair, NE 68009-4459, USA.

SWP-FEB97

Silhouette

SPECIAL EDITION ®

™

That's My Baby!

April 1997 **WHAT TO DO ABOUT BABY**
by Martha Hix (SE #1093)
When a handsome lawyer showed up on Carolyn Grant's
doorstep with a toddler in tow, she didn't know what to think.
Suddenly, she had a little sister she'd never known about...and
a *very* persistent man intent on making Caro his own....

June 1997 **HIS DAUGHTER'S LAUGHTER**
by Janis Reams Hudson (SE #1105)
Carly Baker came to widower Tyler Barnett's ranch to help
his fragile daughter—and connected emotionally with the
caring father and tenderhearted girl. But when Tyler's
interfering in-laws began stirring up trouble, would Carly be
forced to give up the man and child she loved?

And in August, be sure to check out...

ALISSA'S MIRACLE
by
Ginna Gray (SE#1117)

He'd told her that he could never have a child, and lovely
widow Alissa Kirkpatrick was so in love with enigmatic
Dirk Matheson that she agreed to a childless marriage. Until
the pregnancy test proved positive....

THAT'S MY BABY!
**Sometimes, bringing up baby can bring
surprises...and showers of love.**

Look us up on-line at: http://www.romance.net

TMBA-A

And the Winner Is...
You!

...when you pick up these great titles
from our new promotion at your
favorite retail outlet this June!

Diana Palmer
The Case of the Mesmerizing Boss

Betty Neels
The Convenient Wife

Annette Broadrick
Irresistible

Emma Darcy
A Wedding to Remember

Rachel Lee
Lost Warriors

Marie Ferrarella
Father Goose

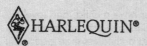

Look us up on-line at: http://www.romance.net   ATWI397-R

Silhouette®

SPECIAL EDITION™

COMING NEXT MONTH

#1111 THE 200% WIFE—Jennifer Greene
That Special Woman!/Stanford Sisters

Abby Stanford always gave 200% to her family, her job...even to making cookies! And when she met Gar Cameron she knew that if he married her, she'd be the *perfect* wife. But Gar didn't want perfection.... He just wanted to love Abby 200%!

#1112 FORGOTTEN FIANCÉE—Lucy Gordon

Amnesiac Justin Hallwood felt inexplicitly drawn to beautiful Sarah Conroy and her toddler son. Would he regain his memory in time to start anew with the woman and child who were so deeply a part of his past?

#1113 MAIL-ORDER MATTY—Emilie Richards

Matty Stewart married her secret crush, Damon Quinn, for the good of his baby girl. But when the infant's custody became uncertain, they had to decide whether love alone could keep them together....

#1114 THE READY-MADE FAMILY—Laurie Paige

Harrison Stone felt trapped when he realized bewitching Isadora Chavez had duped him into marriage to safeguard her younger brother's future. Could this newfound family learn to trust in their hearts—and embrace honest-to-goodness happiness?

#1115 SUBSTITUTE BRIDE—Trisha Alexander

Rachel Carlton had secretly yearned for her twin sister's fiancé for years—and impulsively posed as David Hanson's bride! Now she needed to captivate her unsuspecting "husband" on their week-long honeymoon before the truth came out!

#1116 NOTHING SHORT OF A MIRACLE—Patricia Thayer

Widowed nurse Cari Hallen needed to believe in life—and love—again, and single father Nick Malone needed to open his heart to hope again, too. But it would take nothing short of a miracle to join these two unlikely people together....

From the bestselling author of
Iron Lace and *Rising Tides*

EMILIE RICHARDS

JANET DAILEY
AWARD
WINNER

When had the love and promises they'd shared turned into conversations they couldn't face, feelings they couldn't accept?

Samantha doesn't know how to fight the demons that have come between her and her husband, Joe. But she does know how to fight for something she wants: a child.

But the trouble is Joe. Can he accept that he'll never be the man he's expected to be—and can he seize this one chance at happiness that may never come again?

THE TROUBLE WITH JOE

"A great read and a winner in every sense of the word!"
—Janet Dailey

Available in June 1997
at your favorite retail outlet.

MIRA The brightest star in women's fiction

Look us up on-line at: http://www.romance.net

MER1